THE CLAMOROUS DEAD

Bailiff Mountsorrel Mysteries
Book Four

David Field

SAPERE
BOOKS

THE CLAMOROUS DEAD

Published by Sapere Books.

24 Trafalgar Road, Ilkley, LS29 8HH,
United Kingdom

saperebooks.com

ISBN: 978-0-85495-423-0

1

1596, Nottingham, England

Edward Mountsorrel turned in the saddle and gave the signal for the procession to begin its two-mile journey to Gallows Hill. The driver of the prison cart flicked the reins and the horse jerked forward, throwing the condemned man backwards. They pulled away from the front of the Shire Hall and headed briefly along High Pavement before turning right into Bridlesmith Gate, where a crowd had gathered to watch.

From where he was riding alongside the cart, Edward's colleague, Francis Barton, watched carefully for any sign of public disorder. Amos Hutchins was to be hung for the murder of a man in Malin Hill, well within the town boundary, which was part of Francis's jurisdiction as bailiff to the Sheriff of Nottingham. However, the traditional execution ground on Gallows Hill was outside the town, two miles to the north, which placed it within the jurisdiction of Bailiff Mountsorrel, who served the High Sheriff of Nottinghamshire.

Edward was not normally required to ride at the head of the procession, but a rowdy reaction was expected to Hutchins's demise on the end of the hangman's rope, as he had also committed several other murders while carrying out robberies on the road through the Shire Wood.

With town constables following behind on foot, the cart trundled slowly through the Market Place without any serious disturbance, although the crowd jeered and swore at the condemned man cowering in a corner of the cart, bare-headed and securely bound by ropes.

Amos Hutchins hung his head as the cart halted directly underneath the gallows — two upright beams with a cross-piece from which the rope was already dangling ominously. Public hangman Thomas Gullen stepped solemnly from his grace-and-favour cottage, and for a moment the crowd fell silent as a clergyman muttered a prayer while waving his hand languidly over the condemned man's trembling head.

Amos was then hauled to his feet by two town constables and, following a brief adjustment to the rope to allow for Amos's height, the noose was placed over his head. On a signal from Francis the cart driver flicked the reins and the horse moved forward. Amos's feet scraped along the wooden boards of the cart until his legs were kicking in mid-air, his body spinning slowly as he writhed and choked his last.

Above the jeers, curses and shouts of delight that accompanied Amos's death, a woman's scream pierced the air. A wild creature dressed in what looked like animal skins leaped onto the cart that had been halted to one side and raised her bare arms towards the noonday sun. She bellowed at the top of her voice.

'A thousand curses on you all! A mother will be avenged! This ground shall be forever haunted by the restless spirit of my son, who will bring terrible visitations down upon you all! His soul will live on! A curse be on those who have brought my only son to this end!'

'Seize her!' Edward yelled to Francis as the woman jumped down from the cart. The two bailiffs ran forward as she headed for a dense copse of trees that ended in a sheer drop above a series of old caves carved from the sandstone outcrop on which the execution site stood.

Francis, noting that Edward was seeking to cut the woman off before she could reach the safety of the caves, opted to follow her straight through the copse into which she'd vanished like a hare being pursued by a pack of hounds. His foot caught on a protruding tree root, and with a curse he fell headlong into brushwood that scratched his face. He quickly regained his footing and looked in vain for the fleeing wild woman.

He came to the far side of the copse, where he gazed down on a puzzled-looking Edward, who was staring back up at him.

'Did she come past you?' Francis asked breathlessly.

Edward shook his head. 'No. I had assumed that you had caught her. As it is, she seems to have vanished into thin air.'

'That can't be right,' said Francis, frowning. 'Let's go back through the trees and see if she's hiding in the undergrowth.'

An hour later they came back out at the gallows, where Hutchins's stiffening corpse was still twisting lifelessly in the slight breeze. Thomas Gullen was preparing to cut him down.

'Did that wild woman come this way?' Edward demanded.

Gullen shook his head. 'No, Masters. I thought you must've caught her.'

Edward and Francis exchanged an uneasy glance.

'Quite remarkable how she seems to have disappeared without trace,' said Francis.

'True,' Edward agreed. 'But even more remarkable is that Amos Hutchins was raised as an orphan.'

2

'Two bailiffs, four constables, and *still* the wretched woman got away!' Sheriff William Kniveton bellowed at the two men who stood before the table in the morning room of his grand house in High Pavement, three doors down from St Mary's Church and almost across the road from the Shire Hall in which Edward was based.

Edward would not ordinarily be exposed to the wrath of the joint Sheriff of Nottingham — that was Francis's burden, and Edward would normally only be answerable to the county sheriff, Sir John Byron. But Kniveton had demanded the presence of both men, and, strictly speaking, Edward knew he bore equal blame with Francis for their failure in what should have been the simple task of apprehending a woman in broad daylight.

'Thanks to your ineptitude, a witch has been allowed to spread alarm among the townspeople! What explanation can you offer for your failure?'

'She disappeared into thin air,' Francis mumbled. 'I had her firmly in my view until I tripped and fell, and when I regained my footing there was no sign of her among the trees into which I'd pursued her. I assumed that she'd made it down to the caves below, but Bailiff Mountsorrel was down there, and swears that she never came out of the trees.'

'And there is no proof that she was a witch,' Edward added.

Kniveton thumped his fist down on the table at which he was seated. 'Of *course* she was a witch!' he screeched. 'She disappeared into thin air, according to Barton here. That's a sure sign of witchcraft. And then there was her curse,

8

threatening retribution in the form of ghostly visitations on Gallows Hill!'

'That should keep the numbers down at future executions,' Edward offered in an effort to lighten the proceedings.

'Is *that* how you go about your duties, Mountsorrel? With such flippancy and disregard for the evils that lurk among us? I shall advise your employer of your attitude, with a request that you be replaced before you entirely corrupt Barton. Such Reformist attitudes have only got worse since the abolition of the old religious practices that kept the Devil and all his busy slaves at bay. You are both dismissed to go about your duties, but I want a permanent Town Watch put in place on Gallows Hill. By that I mean both day *and* night! Now get out of my sight, the pair of you!'

'Sorry you had to be there,' Francis muttered as he and Edward strolled through Weekday Cross on their way back towards their respective houses in Whitefriars Lane. They had once shared the house that Francis, a bachelor, now occupied along with an all-purpose houseboy, Ralph, but when Edward had married Elizabeth the couple had bought a piece of vacant land across the road and built their own house. It was a pleasant spot, with plenty of garden ground behind it, and Edward and Francis found it convenient to be so close to each other, given that their duties so frequently overlapped.

'I wasn't aware that I had a choice,' Edward said with a grimace, 'since I was summoned by a personal messenger sent to my house, and told that failure to attend would be reported as dereliction of duty. But you have my sympathy, working for Kniveton. He seems obsessed by the supposed threat of witchcraft.'

'That's because of who his friends are,' Francis told him. 'His almost constant companion is the current vicar of St Mary's, which overshadows his house in more senses than one. Robert Aldridge is "High Church" in his observances, and if his detractors are to be believed he's also a secret Papist. They refuse to shed themselves of the old beliefs — that Satan's disciples walk among us. Aldridge narrowly escaped loss of office after his error in appointing John Darrell as his curate.'

'Why is that name familiar to me?' Edward asked as they turned the corner and headed across the open Greyfriars Green.

Francis snorted. 'I am not surprised that you remember the name. Darrell claimed to have performed an exorcism on William Sommers — the unfortunate lad who suffered from fits. Darrell claimed that the youth was possessed by the Devil, but friends of the boy's father were able to prove that his ailment was born of bad humours. Darrell was exposed as a mountebank and removed from office by the Archbishop of Canterbury, no less. Aldridge and his supporters still rankle about that, and unfortunately for me, one of those who brought about Darrell's downfall was Sheriff George Stokely.'

Edward sighed. 'Whoever decided that Nottingham should have two sheriffs at the same time has a lot to answer for, and it's doubly unfortunate that the two men cannot work more harmoniously for the public good.'

'It's understandable,' Francis observed. 'Unlike Kniveton, Stokely is firmly committed to the "new" form of worship, given his friendship with the mayor and the need to promote his wool business among the wealthy mercers that dominate our Corporation. Were we to make enquiry of him, he would no doubt pour scorn on the very idea that the woman we failed to apprehend was a witch.'

'How can you possibly work for two men who are so far apart in their philosophies?' Edward asked.

Francis chuckled. 'I do what you would no doubt do in my place. I refer matters to the most appropriate of them. For example, if I have a burglary from a shop or workplace to report, I do so to Stokely, confident in the knowledge that he will authorise the most rigorous investigation, sparing no expense. If, on the other hand, someone has been stealing stones from the ruins of an abbey, I can be assured that Kniveton will be most assiduous in ensuring the securing of the thief.' Francis heaved a sigh. 'But his latest instruction has left me with a thankless task, since most of my constables are of the old beliefs, and even those with less gullibility will baulk at having to patrol an execution site at dead of night, particularly given the wild tales that are told of what goes on in those sandstone caves under the cover of darkness. Then there's the fact that I only have six constables, four of whom will be taken up in patrolling Gallows Hill in pairs, since they will hardly be induced to do so alone.'

'I could lend you two of my constables,' Edward offered, 'since Gallows Hill lies, strictly speaking, in the county and therefore under my jurisdiction.'

Francis shook his head. 'I thank you for the gracious offer, but I intend to make it known to Stokely that thanks to Kniveton, there will now be fewer men available to oversee the emptying of the alehouses in the lower town once their landlords have had enough for the day. *Then* we shall see the fur fly between them!'

Edward chuckled. 'I thank God that I have only one man to whom to report, and that he is largely absorbed in the task of converting the former abbey at Newstead that he acquired at a scandalously low price into a family home. Sir John Byron is far less demanding of my time than those who preceded him. I almost dread the expiry of his year of office, for fear that he will be replaced by someone more determined to leave his mark as a preserver of the public peace.'

'I cannot wait to be rid of my two,' Francis complained. 'But as you rightly surmise, there may be even worse to follow them. Anyway, here we are, and I must see what Ralph has left by way of my dinner. Today is his day for visiting his widowed mother in Sneinton.'

'Then you must dine with us,' Edward insisted. 'Elizabeth is forever complaining that we never entertain guests, and Meg's cooking has ever been to your liking.'

'If you are sure that it would not be an imposition,' Francis said with a smile, 'then I should be delighted.'

The two men made their way down the side of the house and into the garden at the rear, where a small girl could be seen sitting among Edward's parsnip rows. She was explaining to her cloth doll how her Daddy had put the seeds in the ground, then watered them every day until their green shoots began to pale, and would soon be digging them carefully out of the ground to give to Mamma, who'd make a delicious stew with them, adding a neck of lamb to the mix if she had any.

Margaret Mountsorrel, named after a grandmother she would never know, was remarkably bright for a child of almost four years of age. Her father's pride and joy, she was a constant source of consolation to her mother Elizabeth, who was beset with the problems presented by their second child, Robert, who, at just over two years old, had still hardly spoken a word, would rarely eat and seemed not to require any sleep.

Margaret gave a cry of delight as she looked up and spied their visitor. Abandoning her doll in the dirt, she scrambled to her feet and ran towards Francis with outstretched arms. The smile on Francis's face was just as wide as he scooped her up and swung her round like a windmill blade.

'How's my little angel today?'

'Mamma told me off,' Margaret complained loudly as her face creased in disapproval.

'And little wonder!' came Elizabeth's voice from the scullery door. 'She pulled Robert's hair when he tried to play with the toy horse that you made her. Thank you for bringing my husband home for his first dinner this week.' She smiled warmly at Francis. 'The least I can do is to invite you to share it with us.'

'I already did,' Edward told her. 'So what can he look forward to eating along with the last of that strong ale we were given by Matthew Brewer?'

'Not above bribery, then,' Francis jested.

Edward smiled. 'Let's just say that I was able to reunite him with the several hogsheads that his apprentice had sold to the landlord of the Black Swan in Bulwell without accounting to Matthew for the money. He was so grateful that he sent round a barrel for the family, and there should still be some left.'

'Despite Edward's best attempt to drink the entirety of the barrel,' Elizabeth teased. 'But come in, and bring your goddaughter with you.'

Margaret all but pushed her father off the bench in her enthusiasm to sit next to Francis. Elizabeth laughed lightly and chided Francis.

'You would make such a good father, and yet you forswear the married state. Why do you not make some fortunate lady your wife, in order that the world can be blessed with little Bartons who can play with their neighbours the little Mountsorrels?'

Francis smiled back. 'In truth, the smell of that delicious pigeon pie that lies before us causes me to reflect that my household ought perhaps to be blessed with someone whose cooking prowess exceeds that of Ralph. He is excellent at keeping the dust from the rushes, but seems destined to tip most of it into his pies. But truth to tell, I have yet to meet the woman who could tolerate my habits, any more than I could tolerate her scolding.'

'Is that what Edward has told you about marriage?' Elizabeth asked with a raised eyebrow. 'That it is all about scolding and bad habits? Did he say nothing about the pleasure of awaking each day while lying in loving arms?'

'Francis has discovered that for himself, while bringing temporary joy into the lives of several widows of the town,' Edward smirked, for which he received a dig in the ribs from Elizabeth. None of them had forgotten the brutal murder of the Widow Timberlake, with whom Francis had been having a relationship.

'That's not what I was referring to, as you are both well aware,' Elizabeth said tartly. 'Francis is well overdue the love of a good woman, and a warm family hearth at which small children can gather while he tells them tales of gallant knights and beautiful ladies.'

'When I find such a woman, and such a hearth,' Francis assured them both, 'you shall be the first to know.'

Edward looked across the table at the uneaten portion of pie that Robert was studiously ignoring. 'Has he eaten nothing?' he asked.

Elizabeth shook her head. 'Not since I was able to cut a ripe pear into such small pieces that I could force them into his mouth. And even then, he contrived to spit some of it out over me. I am so fearful that he will simply wither away and die. He seems to be in a world of his own making, as if the spirits have taken possession of him and left me the husk.'

Tears welled in her eyes, and Francis looked down at the table in embarrassment. Edward hugged her to him.

'Perhaps we should consult a physician,' he suggested.

Elizabeth shook her head vigorously. 'He would only apply leeches, or cut his arm to bleed the bad humours from him. I fear that he is too weak even for that. There are days when I truly believe that what he needs is a priest.'

Edward stared at her. 'You surely cannot believe that rubbish? I heard enough of that from Francis's employer, who had us standing before him this morning like beggar boys caught stealing apples from his orchard.'

'Was that because you allowed that witch to escape?' Elizabeth asked. 'It was the talk of the baker's stall on Timber Hill that she cursed everyone attending Amos Hutchins's hanging, then disappeared in a cloud of smoke. At least, that's what Meg reported on her return.'

'Nothing of the sort,' Francis replied hastily. 'It is true that some old crone began shouting against the injustice of the hanging, and threatened that the souls of the dead would return to haunt Gallows Hill, but she was merely disordered in her wits, so far as I could determine.'

'And you are a physician?' Elizabeth asked sarcastically.

Francis shook his head. 'No, but neither am I one of those credulous Papists who believe in witches and curses. The woman was deranged, that's all.'

'Or possessed,' Elizabeth argued. 'And if you and Edward go in search of her, will she not bring maledictions down on us all? Perhaps she already has — just look at poor little Robert!' She burst into sobs and ran from the chamber with her hand over her mouth.

Her cries of misery could be heard even from the garden into which she had retreated, and when Meg peered cautiously into the main room from the scullery entrance, Edward bid her, 'Look to your mistress, while I see to the clearing of the table.'

3

The following morning Edward pushed open the door to his chamber in the basement of the Shire Hall to find Francis waiting for him with a glum countenance.

'It's started already,' Francis complained. 'The two constables I sent to Gallows Hill came back gibbering wrecks, and hauled me out of bed. Since the bed was not my own, a certain lady in Halifax Lane was most put out that I had confided my intended overnight sojourn to my watch.'

'Serves you right for boasting, if it was the Widow Metcalfe,' Edward replied without sympathy. 'Do I take it that your men were discomforted by ghostly activities?'

'You may, and it is now the talk of the Muster Room that night duties at Gallows Hill are to be avoided at all costs. Since it lies outside the town anyway, they have valid grounds for refusing duty there. Which is why I am here at this ungodly hour. Do you have something warming for my stomach?'

'There's brandy in the cupboard behind you,' Edward told him, 'and you'll find my mug in the drawer of the desk. Are you now prepared to accept that Gallows Hill lies outside your jurisdiction, and that Sheriff Kniveton was out of order in instructing you to organise the patrol up there?'

Francis smiled. 'If you're offering to replace my men with yours, then I accept before you have the opportunity to decline.'

'I don't recall saying that,' Edward corrected him. 'What I *am* saying is that Gallows Hill lies within my remit, and that I shall accordingly arrange to keep watch on events up there.'

'In person?' Francis asked disbelievingly. 'Is this the same man whose wife accused him only yesterday of bringing Hellfire and Damnation down on the family by angering witches?'

'First of all, the woman at Amos Hutchins's execution was no witch, as any man with a rational brain in his head could attest,' Edward replied. 'Secondly, Elizabeth was brought up by pious parents who so instilled the fear of Hell into her that rationality never had a chance, not even when our worthy queen insisted on continuing the good work of her father and brother in closing the door forever on blind faith and superstitious balderdash. In a word, Elizabeth's head knows the truth, but her heart fears the worst.'

'And yet, knowing this, you intend to expose yourself to more recrimination by sticking your head in the witch's cauldron?'

'Did I say that I would be foolhardy enough to tell my wife my intentions?'

Francis gave a hollow laugh. 'So much for the sanctity of the married state that you and Elizabeth were seeking to sell me yesterday at dinner. The bonds of matrimony clearly do not encompass the husband telling the wife what he is about.'

'You will find that this is how so many marriages survive,' Edward said with a grin. 'Now to the business that brought you here. What did your men report?'

Francis sighed. 'The predictable: phantom lights, moaning noises, a disembodied skull floating in mid-air among those trees that we chased the woman through on the day of Hutchins's hanging. The clanking of chains. The chanting of devils as they stoked the fires of Hades. In short, the usual accoutrements of a haunted graveyard.'

'Precisely!' said Edward. '*Exactly* what their overheated imaginations prescribed that they would see and hear. The next watch up there must consist of mature and rational men of the so-called "new" religion, and not a couple of bug-eyed boys who probably believe that angels can flutter down their chimneys.'

Francis snorted. 'I sent Bolton and Ridley, both men well into their thirties; in fact, Ridley will be forty next year, if he lives that long. He is a churchwarden at St Peter's, while Bolton has the imagination of a bullock. They both reported back precisely what they saw, without any attempt at embellishment. All the same, they have asked to be relieved of future duty there, citing the fact that it is not within the town.'

'All the more reason why it should be myself, accompanied by two of my own constables, who undertake further night patrols there,' Edward insisted.

Francis shook his head. 'As I recall, Sheriff Kniveton ordered *me* to investigate and report back to him on the likely whereabouts of the woman who cursed the gallows and all those who attend to its proper functioning. Should it transpire that the same was conducted by the Bailiff of the County, my arse might be found protruding from the window of his front parlour for the entertainment and edification of those progressing along High Pavement.'

'God forbid!' Edward said with a chuckle. 'Assuming that what I just heard was Francis Barton volunteering to accompany me on my patrol of Gallows Hill, then I accept.'

'When do you propose we go?' Francis asked.

Edward frowned. 'Not this coming night. I have enough to cause me unease for one day, given the need to travel to Newstead Hall.'

'Sir John also wishes to learn more about the goings-on at Gallows Hill?'

'Probably, but equally probably not. He's normally content with my appearance on his hallowed doorstep once a month or so, but for some reason he sent a messenger after dinner yesterday, with a summons north.'

'What might be his reason for summoning you, then, if not the disgraceful display at the hanging?' Francis asked.

Edward shrugged. 'Who knows? It certainly won't be to thank me for my hard work in keeping the county law-abiding. He only issues a summons for my attendance when he has something to complain about.'

'So when shall we venture to Gallows Hill?'

'My immediate thought is that we should leave it for a few days, then make enquiry of Thomas Gullen regarding whether or not his sleep has been disturbed by ghostly visitors. Given that his cottage is situated only a few feet from the gallows itself, and that his is the hand that has dispatched so many to their doom, he must surely be the one the demonic forces are most anxious to torment. I'm surprised that he hasn't made a complaint already.'

'It's only been a day since the curse was laid,' Francis reminded him. 'I was surprised that it manifested itself so soon afterward.'

'If indeed it did,' Edward commented, at which Francis seemed to take offence.

'You imply that my constables were being untruthful regarding what they saw? If so, feel free to take a short walk down to the Guildhall and speak to them yourself, if they haven't gone home already. Neither of them has ever been known to be affected by liquor while on duty. In fact, Ridley has sworn against liquor of any sort.'

'I don't suggest for one moment that your men were either intoxicated or reporting falsely,' Edward assured him. 'What I *am* suggesting is that what they saw was laid on for their benefit, so that word would get out that the curse had begun to take effect.'

'And what purpose would that serve?' Francis challenged him.

'Precisely the purpose it has *already* served,' Edward replied. 'Tales spreading throughout the county that we have evil spirits lurking around our execution site, ready to drag the unwary down to Hell.'

'What if Gullen resigns as hangman as the result of all this?' Francis speculated as the dreadful prospect struck him. 'His is not the most sought-after position, after all. Is there not a risk that we'll lose his services if we aren't seen to deal with the problem?'

'What do you have in mind?' Edward asked. 'An exorcism? How good are you with bell, book and candle? Come to think of it, that sort of flummery is proscribed these days, so you'd need to seek to drive off the demons with your club, and perhaps a few well chosen words.'

'Why do I get the feeling that you're not taking this as seriously as you ought?' Francis demanded.

'Because I don't believe in ghosts, demons, witches or the dead rising from their graves,' said Edward. 'And neither should you, if we're to expose the pretence for what it is — the dishonest taking advantage of the gullible, just like John Darrell pretending to expel demons from the head of that poor lad William Sommers.'

'And how do you propose that we establish the truth, even assuming that you're right?'

'By noting carefully what manifestations occur at night, then returning by day to make careful examination of the ground for signs of legerdemain.'

'And what precisely is *that*, pray?'

'Conjuring — sleight of hand — the sort of trickery employed by mountebanks at country fairs, to charm the gullible out of their shillings.'

'Dice cogging may be one thing,' Francis objected, 'but that is hardly in the same league as producing phantoms from thin air, or causing the dead to rise from their graves.'

'Do you recall that band of wandering players you ran out of town several years ago?'

'Of course, since they were attracting pickpockets and prostitutes. In fact, I suspected that they were part of their company. But what is your point?'

'Well, when they left here they headed north, and my sheriff at that time — William Sutton, as I recall — gave specific instruction that they be allowed to ply their trade in the local villages, in order to distract folk from the famine that was imminent. I had occasion to watch them present a spectacle on the green in front of Nuthall Mill. It was all about dragons, the heroism of St George, the rescue of fair damsels and the ascent from Hell of the very Devil himself. It was all achieved by skilful illusion such as lies within the capabilities of only a few. Before we subscribe to the general belief that we are being besieged by the tormented souls of those condemned to Purgatory, I suggest we look more closely for signs of similar trickery and deception — illusions that persuade the eyes to see that which is not there.'

Francis had no answer to that other than a slow shake of the head. Then another thought struck him. 'What do we tell Gullen in the meantime?'

'Nothing, unless he complains, then we share our suspicions with him, and seek his assistance.'

'And if by some miracle he does *not* complain?'

'Then we know who is responsible. Or at least we will know that those behind this business have recruited him to play his part.'

'It's all too fanciful for my taste,' Francis complained.

'No less fanciful than the possibility of the dead rising from their graves, or witches descending in the night on their besoms. Anyway, it is time that I took the road to Newstead, given that it's half a day's ride. Wish me luck. You at least have the more pleasant task of advising your constables that there will be no more nightly patrols of Gallows Hill — for them, anyway.'

4

'I want you to find me a witch,' Sir John Byron declared as he strode purposefully from his elegant dining room into the side chamber, leaving his dinner unfinished.

Edward had hardly expected to be invited to join his employer in his main meal of the day, but was a little startled that whatever the High Sheriff of Nottinghamshire had in mind was sufficiently important to have caused the renowned gormandiser to rise from his meal. He was even more concerned that it was to be left to him to resolve.

'Take a seat,' Byron ordered, as he did likewise and began to expand on his earlier instruction. 'Not just any witch, mind you — the one who's been bedevilling my estate. Identify her, locate her, find evidence of her devilry, then bring her back to the Hall for a good bonfire to be made of her foul carcass.'

Edward racked his brain for any memory regarding the rumoured activities of a witch in the vicinity of what had, until recent years, been the extensive grounds of an Augustinian abbey. Some forty years previously it had been closed down by order of Thomas Cromwell, acting for the late King Henry. Sir John's father had acquired both the abbey buildings and their picturesque surroundings, complete with a lake into which, according to local legend, had been thrown many rich artefacts belonging to the dissolved holy house.

The 'Hall' to which Sir John pompously referred was what was left of the once extensive abbey, large parts of which had been in a ruinous state when his father had purchased it and begun a series of extensions and improvements that had rendered the main portion of 'Newstead Hall' at least habitable. Sir John was continuing the work, and harboured hopes that it would eventually be graced by a visit from Her Majesty, if she lived long enough to see the former abbey transformed into a residence grand enough to rival Wollaton Hall, the family seat of his nearest neighbours and unspoken rivals, the Willoughbys.

'What makes you think that a witch has set her sights on your fine home?' Edward asked politely.

'It's obvious,' Byron replied testily. 'Several of my tenants' cattle have recently died from a mysterious pestilence, the harvest was poorer than the previous year, and one of the coachman's dogs was found recently with its throat ripped out.'

'All of those events, unfortunate as they are, could be explained away on grounds other than witchcraft,' Edward observed, earning a responding snort from Byron.

'You know, of course, that the former prior cursed this place before he slunk away with his grubby pension from the Crown?'

'No, I was not aware of that,' Edward conceded. Rational argument was unlikely to win the day on this occasion.

'Then presumably you are also unaware of sightings of a ghostly monk in and around the ground floor rooms?'

'Indeed not,' Edward confirmed as his heart sank further. 'Do you believe this monk, and the curse, to be associated with the unfortunate incidents to which you referred? If so, why do you also have cause to suspect the malice of a witch?'

'Surely you will be aware that one of the ways in which witches go about their evil schemes is to feed off any ghostly humours that may surround a place? In any case, I have it on good report that the hag in question may be found living not an hour away from here, in the direction of Papplewick. She prospered in the days of my father, it seems, by selling amulets to ward off evil spirits to those who were working to restore this house, and would regularly encounter the "Black Monk", as he is known. Of course, I gave word that there was to be no more such trading of worthless trinkets, and was subsequently advised that she cursed me and mine. It was shortly after receiving that warning that the beasts began dying, and the crops to wither in the ground.'

'And you now wish me to locate her, and somehow acquire proof that it is she who lies behind these misfortunes?' Edward asked, in the hope that he might have misheard the original instruction.

Byron shot him a baleful glare. 'Did I not already say so? These agents of the Devil must be rooted out and burned. Not hanged — *burned*! It is the only way to purge the evil from them. The Scottish King James learned that during his time in Denmark, where he made a detailed study of the matter. In Scotland he's succeeded in burning many such possessed prostitutes of Satan. In England we have allowed them the mercy of a hanging.'

'That is, of course, no reason for the authorities here in England to put to death those who are falsely accused of being witches,' Edward argued, then wished he hadn't as he saw Byron's face flush crimson.

'You dare to suggest I am making false accusation?' he roared. 'It is for *you* to find me the evidence I require in order to have this pestilence removed from my doorstep, which is why I summoned you here. Either perform your duties, or I shall appoint someone who *can*! Now lose no more time in the matter — ride hard to Papplewick and find the woman.'

'Do you know her name?' Edward asked as civilly as he could.

'Those who foolishly purchased the amulets from her referred only to "Magic Mary", and it would seem that she occupies a cave somewhere along a riverbank. She should not be hard to track down. By posing as someone seeking her services, you may soon ensnare her into an admission of dealings with the Devil that will justify her death. Have you partaken of dinner, by the way? It is said that these matters are best not tackled on an empty stomach.'

'As it transpires, I have not,' Edward replied as he glanced through the still open door at the salvers of meat that adorned the sheriff's dining table. 'I left the town at an early hour to be in time for our meeting.'

'Very well,' Byron replied as he rose from his chair. 'If you go down to the kitchen and tell the cook that I gave you authorisation, she should be in the process of feeding the remainder of the household, and you may join them.'

Two hours later Edward found himself approaching a crude shelter on the bank of a wide stream that did not quite qualify as a river, but which was swirling through a river meadow heavy with wildflowers and full of birdsong. The front of the shelter looked more like an apothecary's shopfront, with plants of all description hanging in garlands, and a mortar and pestle sitting on a wide tree trunk.

The woman who sat watching his approach looked as if she had grown to maturity as part of the natural world by which she was surrounded, given her long green gown that appeared to have been woven from broad leaves, the cap on her head that could have been crafted from soft tree bark, and the dark brown facial features so familiar to him from the many travelling people he had encountered in the past, and frequently moved on following complaints from villagers. Such hair as was visible beneath the cap was as white as snow, but the challenging twinkle from the blue eyes that met his as he dismounted suggested that she was much younger.

'I seek Magic Mary,' Edward announced.

The woman smiled. 'And you believe that I am she?'

'I am certain of it,' he replied with a smile of his own. 'I have never seen so many plants and other signs of natural physick in the one place, other than in a herbalist's premises in a busy town, and this is clearly no busy town.'

'You require a simple for that headache?' she asked, and he was surprised that the nagging pain at the back of his skull that had dogged him all day was so obvious to a casual observer.

'You have one?' he asked, opting to humour her.

'I would not have enquired otherwise,' she replied with an authoritative air that reminded him of one of the Holy Brothers who had taught him during his orphanage days. 'Sit yourself down on that tree stump while I prepare you a mixture of feverfew and willow bark. I will add honey to make it more acceptable to your palate, since left to itself it can have a bitter flavour.'

She reached for her mortar and pestle, took a handful of what looked like flower petals, and ground them into a paste before adding a sprinkling of what appeared to be tree bark. As she worked, she asked casually, 'You are here to arrest me as a witch?'

Edward's jaw dropped in astonishment. Before he could speak, however, she said, 'Your master has heard that I dabble in the Black Arts, having given my soul to the Devil?'

'Sir John has reason to be concerned over the recent loss of some of his tenants' cattle.'

'And he blames *me* for that?' she asked, greatly amused. 'Why does he not blame those of his tenants who allow their beasts to wander at will, eating whatever attracts their eye? The boggy ground around his lake contains much dropwort — "water hemlock" as it is known — and cattle are attracted to its broad leaves and fleshy roots. Tell him to fence off his lake and fishponds and there will be no more poisoned cattle.'

'He spoke also of a dog found with its throat ripped out,' Edward added.

She stared at him for a moment, then gently shook her head. 'Are you so much of a town man that you have never heard of wolves or wild hogs?'

'I am enough of a country man to know that wolves have long since been banished from this land.'

'And there you would be making a false assumption,' she replied confidently. 'True it is that they were ruthlessly hunted in former times, but that simply made those that survived more cunning and desperate. They compete with house dogs for food, and when they come across one, well, naturally they kill it. There are at least two wolves still loose in this area of the country, and on still nights you can sometimes hear them howling in the woods. No doubt the feeble-minded and gullible mistake them for the souls of those in Purgatory.'

'Like the feeble-minded and gullible that you once sold amulets to, to ward off evil spirits?'

The woman held out a wooden pot, into which she had decanted the mixture. 'Drink this now, before its potency wears off. As for the amulets, they served a purpose.'

'The purpose of making you rich, you mean?'

'Take a look around my humble dwelling, and *then* assess how wealthy I am. Drink the remainder of that in one swallow, including the gritty bits that may stick in your throat.' She looked him up and down. 'I deduce from your bearing that you either are, or once were, a man at arms. Am I correct?'

'You are, but what of it?'

'Would you ever contemplate going into battle without armour?'

'Of course not, if there was armour available.'

'But the armour did not make you a better fighter, did it?'

'No, but it gave me the courage to fight in the first place.'

'Precisely. And if you were fearful of evil spirits, and I gave you an amulet for your protection, it would give you the necessary courage, would it not?'

'But it would not, by your reasoning, make me any stronger in actually fighting those evil spirits, would it?'

'That is where you are wrong.' She smiled knowingly. 'What men choose to call evil spirits are simply illusions sent by dark forces to frighten us, and by this means hold us in thrall to them. They have no *real* power of their own, but merely employ the simple fears of the unenlightened in order to control their actions. If I wished to prevent you entering my house, for example, I would lead you to believe that it contains a demon. It doesn't, but if you believe that it does, then you will not dare enter. But if I give you a simple binding for your wrist, made from sturdy vines, and tell you that it will protect you from that demon, you are more inclined to suppress your fear and enter.'

'So the amulets that you sold were no different from the pondwater that mountebanks sell at country fairs as magical potions that will make their wives fertile, or cure their boils?'

'In one sense, no. They had no power of their own — no magical properties, if you prefer. But on the arm of someone who actually believed in its power, the amulet served to enable them to overcome fear born of superstition, and get on with their appointed task. In the matter to which you refer, they were able to continue with the work of restoring the former priory buildings without fear of the so-called "Black Monk". Sir John should be grateful to me for allowing work to continue on his precious Hall — instead he sends you to seize me to be burned at the stake.'

'How did you know that?' Edward demanded.

She raised an eyebrow. 'Your headache has melted away, has it not?'

'Indeed it has. Your potion was truly powerful.'

'The truth is that it was not the potion. You believed in its power, and your body did the rest. If you prefer, I weaved my magic over you, and drove the pain from your head. But would you call such magic "evil"?'

'Of course not. You can cure all ailments by this … "skill" you possess?'

'A skill we *all* possess, Edward. My mother taught me that, and my younger sister is far more gifted than I. When you are attuned to nature, such things are no longer either wonderful or mysterious. I am regularly called upon to cure sickness in infants, deliver babies, help the elderly and dying in their torments, make crops grow, and persuade cattle to yield more milk. They call me a white witch.'

'This does not explain how you know my name, or how you knew my true reason for calling on you today,' Edward persevered.

Her voice dropped to a whisper. 'You have heard of "second sight"?'

'Indeed I have — another sign of the Devil's work, or so it is said.'

She sighed. 'Like every other gift we are given, it may of course be used for either good or evil. Your strong sword arm may be employed either to protect the weak or to persecute them. You may, with the point of your sword, either protect a maid from being violated by one with evil designs on her virtue, or force her to submit to your own vile desires. The power is the same in either case, but the choice is yours.'

'So you claim to employ this "second sight" only for good?'

'I believe that were I to employ that gift for evil, it would be taken from me. I could, had I wished, have made use of your fear regarding your son's health and threatened to curse him further. But had I done so, then I would not have been allowed to learn that you are, in your heart, a good man who shrinks from dragging a helpless woman to an unjust death. I realised I had nothing to fear from you if I dealt with you honestly and openly.'

'As you have done,' Edward confirmed. There was an awkward silence, broken by Edward's hesitant next question. 'What is it about my son that you can tell me?'

'Only that you and your woman worry ceaselessly about his listless humour and his lack of appetite. He is but two years of age or thereby, am I correct?'

'You are.'

'And there is also a girl, a year or two older, who is greatly admired by all who come into her company?'

'Yes,' Edward confirmed. 'His older sister, Margaret. She never fails to bring us joy.'

'And the boy, he sees this?'

'Of course, since we keep close company at all times.'

There was a lengthy silence, at the end of which she rose and selected several herbs from those hanging in profusion behind her, and began grinding them into a powder. This she screwed into a ball and wrapped in a broad leaf, handing the finished item to Edward.

'Place one half of this in a warm drink — perhaps some diluted mulled wine, if your woman will permit a young boy to be given such. It is a fusion of lavender to soothe the mind, and a little foxglove to stimulate the heart. Your boy is, I suspect, suffering from a melancholic humour because he feels that he will never be as precious to you both as is the girl. You must also play your part in assuring him that you and his mother think no less of him than his more ebullient sister.'

'You are most kind,' Edward replied, as he reached for the money bag at his waist.

She reached out and stalled his hand. 'Whatever evil tales may be told about my avarice, my simples come free of charge. It is sufficient that you are not going to take me back to Newstead Hall as a witch. Or are you?'

'Indeed I am not,' Edward said with a reassuring smile. 'But even if I return to my master with the falsehood that I was unable to find you, there may be others who will make it their business to come to your door. Someone who will not shrink from what he perceives to be his duty, guided by another who wishes you ill. You must surely have made enemies over the years?'

She thought for a moment before nodding. 'There is one, for certain. Her name is Agnes Merryweather, and she may be found in neighbouring Hucknall, which lies on your journey

33

back into the town, should I be correct in my feeling that this is where you live.'

'You are correct,' Edward confirmed. 'But why does she wish you ill?'

'It is a long story, but there was a time when I exposed her as a cruel person — one who conducts wicked deeds simply because of the pleasure to be derived therefrom. She had ensnared the heart of a young man called Thomas, who lived in Linby, where we all lived in those days. He had previously been attached to my younger sister Catherine, who was almost bereft of her wits from the grief of losing his affections. I used my powers to lift the scales from his eyes and reveal Agnes for what she was. She has never forgiven me, and would dearly love to see me hung as a witch.'

'What became of your sister and the man she loved?' Edward asked.

'They married the following year, and had a happy life together until he was taken by that most recent contagion that accounted for so many. I was powerless against it, and Catherine now lives as a widow close by Arnold, still tending the fruit farm that she and Thomas established there.'

'If you are still in danger of betrayal by this woman, why do you not move away?'

'Where would I go?' she asked as she indicated the various items by which they sat surrounded. 'I have no wagon, and even were I able to move all these things that are precious to me, who would take me in?'

'What about your widowed sister in Arnold? Would she not be prepared to give you sanctuary?'

'Perhaps, although I would need to enquire of her, and I have no means of travelling from here other than by foot. It is a long walk from Papplewick to Arnold.'

'But a short ride,' Edward said. 'If your sister might offer you sanctuary, the least I can do is return here with a wagon, and remove you completely from any possibility of danger.'

She leaned forward and kissed his cheek. 'My instincts did not betray me. You are indeed a good man, and it shall be as you suggest. In truth, I grow lonely here, never having married, and to be reunited with my sister would bring some light into my otherwise dreary existence. Her name is Catherine Fellows, and she may be found along the track that leads from the marketplace in Arnold towards the village of Daybrook. She does not know me as "Magic Mary", of course. My real name is Rose — Rose Middleham.'

5

'I hope you've been urging Francis to do something about those horrible goings-on at Gallows Hill,' Elizabeth announced as she kissed Edward perfunctorily on the cheek. He had just walked into the all-purpose downstairs room after removing his muddy boots in the doorway.

'We agreed to share that responsibility, if you recall. And I've spent the day with Sheriff Byron, who insists that I smoke out a witch living close to his estate.'

'And did you?'

'No, as it transpires. Is there any of that wine left?'

'A little, why? And don't seek to change the subject — why must you bring curses down on this family by hunting witches?'

'I haven't, as I think I just explained. There was no sign of the woman when I went in search of her. As for the wine, I thought I might warm some up and have it with my supper.'

'I wasn't referring to Sir John's witch,' said Elizabeth. 'I meant the one who cursed Gallows Hill. The stories about that place get worse by the day. Ghostly faces suspended in mid-air. Disembodied voices calling through the trees. The flames of Hell rising up through the ground. Clanking chains and…'

'You really shouldn't believe all the nonsense that Meg brings back from the Market Place,' Edward insisted. 'Once these wild tales go into circulation, they just get more and more exaggerated with the telling. There's almost certainly a simple explanation.'

'The "simple explanation", as you call it, is that we are being cursed for our wickedness,' Elizabeth retorted as tears began to well in her eyes. 'Not just yours and mine, but *everyone's*. God will smite us like he did Sodom and Gomorrah.'

'You're beginning to sound like a parson,' Edward complained. 'And if indeed God is intending to smite us, why does he employ witches and demons? Why not angels?'

She had no answer, but he was curious as to what had provoked this unaccustomed outburst from a woman he had always known to be so level-headed and calm. And for that matter, so dismissive of the sorts of superstitions that came from religious excess.

'Are these your own private fears, or are you simply repeating what others are saying? Are you speaking for yourself or credulous creatures like Meg?'

'Both, I suppose,' she conceded.

'That's what you're intended to think, *all* of you. Whoever is organising these false displays is seeking to spread fear and despondency throughout the town.'

'Why?' she challenged him, but he shook his head.

'I have no idea at present, but it falls to Francis and myself to find out.'

'I forbid you to go anywhere near that awful place!' she cried out, before adding, 'What I mean is, think of us before you do so. I do not presume to order you around, but to take on the forces of evil is to risk your very soul, and those of the people who mean the most to you.'

'I'm well aware of that,' Edward reassured her as he led her gently to the table, where Meg was laying out the dried herring, cheese, bread and fruit for their supper. Elizabeth sat down next to Margaret, while Edward lifted Robert from the floor where he'd been silently watching them with a blank expression on his face. 'As for you, precious little man,' he said as he lowered Robert onto the bench next to him, 'it's time you learned how much Mamma and Daddy love you, and how important you are to us. Daddy will even share his wine with you, if Meg would be so good as to warm up some of whatever is left over, and bring two mugs to the table.'

A few minutes later, while Elizabeth was busy supervising the cutting of cheese into suitably small portions for Margaret, Edward surreptitiously slipped half the simple he'd acquired from Rose Middleham into the mug in front of Robert, and invited the boy to join him in 'a toast to Daddy's success in fighting off the bad people!'

Elizabeth looked on with disapproval as Robert imitated Edward's actions, lifting the mug to his lips, tipping the contents into his mouth, then putting it down hastily as his eyes bulged and he spat out a small amount of the mulled liquid.

'*Really*, Edward!' Elizabeth admonished him. 'It's bad enough that you're teaching our son to drink at such a young age, but clearly he has no taste for stale wine.'

'He must get used to the taste, if he is to grow up as strong and fearless as his father,' Edward insisted as he helped himself to a piece of dried fish and cut several slices of bread, taking one of them and placing the fish on top of it in order to consume both items at once.

'Let's at least hope that he doesn't develop your terrible manners at board,' Elizabeth responded with a shake of her head, then stared in amazement as Robert reached out for one of the remaining slices of bread and stuffed it into his mouth with a grin.

'He's begun already — look!' she declared in a shaky voice.

Robert swallowed his first voluntary morsel, smiled back across the table and said, 'Mamma tell Daddy off.'

Margaret burst into shrieks of laughter, while Edward said a silent prayer of thanks to a wise woman half a day's ride away.

'Kniveton's not happy,' Francis announced as he looked up from his desk in the Guildhall.

'Nothing, I suspect, will make him happy unless we bring in some hapless old lady and string her up in the Market Place,' replied Edward. 'Although Byron would probably argue that she should be burned.'

'That wouldn't stop the incidents, though, would it?' Francis replied gloomily. 'I have two constables on the point of resigning to become farm labourers rather than face going up to Gallows Hill on night duty. So how are things with you?'

'Dreadful, in one sense, but very hopeful in another. Which news do you want first?'

'The bad — then at least I'll have the good news to lighten my mood.'

'Very well, then. The bad news is that even Elizabeth, who's normally so tolerant of other people, and has no deep Catholic persuasion of which I'm aware, seems convinced that the portals of Hell have opened here in Nottingham, and that "someone" — by which I rather gather she means you — should be doing something about it. Quite *what* exactly, she was unable to advise me, but it's apparent that the entire town is now convinced that the woman at Amos Hutchins's hanging has unleashed all the forces of darkness upon the place. The *other* bad news is that Byron seems to think that he also has a witch bedevilling his estate, and he sent me in search of her.'

'Did you find her?'

'That's the good news. I came across a kind lady living by the riverside in Papplewick, who's regarded as something of a wise woman locally. However, as we both know, this could soon lead to her being condemned as a witch if she gets on the wrong side of those who wish her ill. I need to borrow a wagon so that I can help her remove herself to the safety of her sister's property before Byron finds her.'

'And why would you take that risk, just for some old lady who could probably give you agues and boils if you displeased her?'

'That's the rest of the good news, Francis! She is also blessed with the second sight, and she was able to tell me all about Robert's sad humour, his refusal to eat and so on. Then she gave me a simple which I dropped into some wine last night, and tricked him into drinking. He not only ate some bread without any prompting, but he also spoke for the first time — real words, not just the occasional grunt that we are used to hearing from him. I do believe that this woman, and her potions, may be the secret to his recovery from whatever has been ailing him.'

'And that's why you want to rescue this old lady from Byron's clutches?'

'She's *not* an old lady, at least not in most people's estimation. I doubt if she has yet attained her fortieth year, but she has white hair and dresses oddly. She also lives alone, and is surrounded by herbs and other strange plants that she fashions into simples and potions.'

'Does she by any chance have a cat?' Francis asked with a chuckle. 'Or perhaps a dog, or a goat, or a ferret?'

'Not that I saw,' Edward replied. 'But why might you wish to know?'

'Because you have just described the perfect witch, the confirmation of which would be the presence close by of what the ignorant call her "familiar" — an animal that suckles at her breast, and into which she can transform herself when the need arises. Which would explain how our wild woman on Gallows Hill was able to evade capture.'

'You are not only beginning to sound like my wife,' Edward complained with a frown, 'but you are failing to take the matter seriously. In penance for that, you can accompany me to Papplewick. I shall need one of your wagons anyway.'

'You have wagons of your own,' Francis reminded him, 'and I have much to do here, organising my rapidly diminishing band of constables into a company to suppress the growing disorder in the town while we play at hunting witches.'

'My own wagons are spread across the county,' Edward explained, 'and were I to be seen with one of mine in the region of Papplewick, word would soon travel back to Sheriff Byron that I should be bringing him his witch. On the other hand, a town wagon with a town bailiff might pass for a man seeking to assist his aunt, or perhaps his older sister, to change residences. And as for catching witches, I think that it's high time that you and I paid a visit to Tom Gullen. His cottage lies only feet from where these nightly manifestations are said to occur, and I would be very interested to learn what he has to report regarding them. Does it not strike you as strange that he has thus far made no report of those matters that seem to have ignited the imagination of the entire town?'

'I *had* wondered about that,' Francis confirmed. 'But what has that to do with any journey to Papplewick?'

'That is where we shall travel to after we have spoken to Gullen. We'll be well on our way once we've gone that far out of town. So, unless you can convince me there is something more urgent, let us lose no more time. It promises to be a busy day, and without the benefit of any dinner.'

Thomas Gullen appeared in the doorway to his cottage as they climbed down off the wagon and hitched the horse to the rail. He looked furtively at each of them in turn, and waited for one of them to speak. It was Edward who took the initiative.

'You look alert enough, for one whose sleep must have been disturbed these past few nights.'

His face remained blank as he replied, 'Masters?'

'My constables have recently advised me that as night falls, this place becomes the Devil's playground,' Francis said. 'Did you not feel the need to report that interesting fact?'

'I thought as how your constables would be doing that,' he replied sullenly. 'As for what goes on out here at night, I keep well within me cottage, with me shutters closed.'

'So what is it that you hide from?' Edward asked, hoping to trap him into saying something incriminating.

'I don't rightly know, since I've got me head hidden under me bedclothes. But according to the constables…'

'Yes, yes, I'm fully aware of what the constables are reporting,' Francis replied testily. 'But for all that you can see or hear for yourself, there might as well be a foreign invasion going on out here every night, is that what you're telling us?'

Again the man was not about to be caught out. 'I obviously hears a lot — all that wailing and clanking and suchlike. But when I hears that, I keeps me head down, like I said. I'm not paid to sit and look at ghosts and stuff — just to hang folks.'

A short while later, Francis and Edward rode away, leaving Gullen staring after them from the door of his cottage.

'Well, at least that's one man who's not about to resign from his post,' Francis muttered.

'Did you believe him?' Edward asked. 'The finest show to be seen anywhere in the East Midlands free of charge, and he hides under the bedclothes?'

'He may be genuinely frightened,' Francis pointed out.

'He may also be the man responsible,' Edward insisted. 'I think that the time is almost right for us to return your constables to the more pleasurable tasks of cracking skulls at chucking-out time in the alehouses, and running in doxies plying their trade openly in the streets.'

'You suspect Gullen of being behind all this?'

'He's not got the wit to organise it himself,' Edward conceded. 'But if I'm correct in my belief that this is all a crafty contrivance by those whose true talents lie in the theatre, then they couldn't possibly stage it without Gullen's co-operation. Or, at the very least, his connivance. He very conveniently feigns fear, or at least a failure to look more carefully at what goes on here nightly.'

'And if I judge you aright, you plan to take over the night watch and catch him at it?'

'Not just me, Francis — both of us. Make no plans for tomorrow night, or the night after.'

'Thanks to my men hauling me out of bed in Halifax Lane, there's currently no pliant widow to distract me in that regard. That's been another unfortunate result of the witch's curse.'

Rose Middleham met the two men with a broad smile as they approached her crude hut. She held open the animal hides in her doorway to reveal rows of neatly stacked bundles, and nodded at Edward.

'You kept your promise, then. How did you fare with the simple I gave you?'

'It worked beyond my fondest expectations,' Edward beamed back, 'and I am here in the hope that you can supply me with more.'

'I can, although you must take care not to administer too much at once,' she told him. 'The foxglove can be fatal if taken in excess, and in a young heart it can engender a wild fluttering. But are you not also here with another purpose, or have I packed all my worldly goods in vain?'

'No, you have not,' Edward assured her, 'hence our arrival with a wagon. Allow me to introduce my colleague Francis Barton, bailiff to the Sheriff of Nottingham. It's his wagon and his brawny arm that will assist in the loading of your goods ahead of your transfer to Daybrook.'

Rose looked Francis up and down, and blushed slightly. 'But it is not the strength of his arm that the ladies find so pleasing, is it? I should perhaps say no more about that, however.'

'No, you should not,' Francis agreed as he looked uncomfortably down at the ground. 'Particularly since we have not yet been fully introduced.'

'My oversight,' Edward said, amused at his colleague's embarrassment. 'This lady is Rose Middleham, and she can see through to your very heart. Or a little lower down in your case, apparently.'

'You wish to travel down to Daybrook, I'm advised,' Francis mumbled in an attempt to change the subject. 'Let's get the wagon loaded, then, and be on our way before darkness sets in.'

Three hours later, as the sun began to disappear behind the oaks and birches that formed the eastern fringe of the Shire Wood, they turned left onto the track that led to Daybrook, and Rose guided them into the lane that led to a large orchard containing trees heavy with apples and pears. There was a house largely constructed from log slabs and with a greying thatch in urgent need of renewal. A woman appeared from a barn at the sound of the wagon approaching.

'Kitty!' Rose called out, then leaped down from the front board and embraced her sister.

Catherine looked across at the wagon piled high with Rose's plants and equipment. Her eye lit upon the two men, before she turned to her sister. 'Did you take a husband at long last?'

Rose chuckled. 'No, these men are both bailiffs. The one with the reins in his hand is Edward Mountsorrel, Bailiff of the County. He is here to see me safely into the sanctuary of my sister's house, if she will have me?'

'And why do you need sanctuary?' Catherine asked as her gaze lingered on Francis, who was already lifting items down from the wagon.

'I can explain that,' Edward volunteered. 'My master is the Sheriff of the County, Sir John Byron, and he's got it into his head that his estate is cursed by a witch. He sent me in search of that witch, and suggested that it might be your sister. She is, of course, nothing of the sort, but out of caution I advised her to move away from Papplewick. I also undertook to assist in that move, along with my colleague Francis Barton, bailiff to the Sheriff of Nottingham. So here we are. You *are* Catherine, I assume?'

'I am,' Catherine confirmed, 'but those who wish to know me better call me Kitty. As for you, sister dear, you are more than welcome, particularly since the harvest is almost upon us, and I need every pair of hands I can get to strip the trees and fill the barrels. There are local boys who earn a few pennies daily by assisting in that, but with your gentle hands the fruit will be less bruised.'

'What about *men* with gentle hands?' Francis asked cheekily as he stopped what he'd been doing and walked towards Catherine with a broad smile. 'If you allow me to return another day to handle your fruit, I promise not to leave any bruises.'

'Please excuse my friend,' Edward interjected as Rose smirked and Catherine's face turned red. 'His town duties have somewhat coarsened his manners.'

'I am used to coarseness, living out here in the country,' Catherine said, looking at Francis. 'What I have sadly missed of late, however, is a man's strong arm where it is most needed.'

'I can spare a few days next week, if that would be suitable, Mistress Catherine?' Francis offered, his eyes fixed on her ample upper torso.

'I shall happily anticipate that,' she replied, 'provided that you call me Kitty. The best fruit will be reserved for your experienced hands.'

As the two bailiffs rode back into town on the empty wagon, Edward turned to glare at Francis. 'How can you claim to have a few days free, given all that we must do in order to expose the so-called devilry at Gallows Hill for what it really is?'

'I always have days free for what I have in mind,' said Francis with a leer, 'and you forget that the Widow Metcalfe is no longer welcoming me across her threshold.'

'Just ensure that your dalliance with the Widow Fellows does not complicate our business even more,' Edward warned him. 'But perhaps this time Elizabeth will get her wish, and Francis Barton will become respectably married.'

'The joy somehow goes out of it when I contemplate acting respectably,' Francis said with a laugh.

6

'I suppose Kniveton finds it more satisfying to yell at both of us rather than just you,' Edward muttered as he met Francis on the front steps of the Shire Hall.

As the two men made their reluctant way across High Pavement to Sheriff Kniveton's spacious house in the shadow of St Mary's Church, Francis muttered an apology, adding by way of justification, 'Gallows Hill is within the county, after all, and he no doubt looks to you to assist me.'

'By rights he should never have ordered you to investigate the matter,' Edward replied. 'I'm surprised that Sheriff Byron hasn't challenged that, instead of ordering me to persecute an innocent wise woman.'

'I'm glad he did,' Francis grinned as they announced their business to the steward who answered their knock, 'since it has given me the opportunity to learn all about fruit harvesting.'

Edward chuckled. 'That is without doubt the least likely skill that you will require here in town. The few private orchards that exist, such as the one behind this house and the ones all the way up Stoney Street, are all harvested by kitchen staff. The fruit that you hope to handle in Daybrook comes with most attractive appendages.'

'Go through to the morning room, where my master is expecting you,' the steward instructed them as he opened the door wider to permit them entry. As they walked down the long hallway towards the room at the rear, they heard two male voices. One was unmistakably that of Sheriff Kniveton. Edward muttered an oath as he recognised the other.

They reached the open doorway and halted.

'Come in, both of you,' Kniveton instructed them, then gestured towards the man seated to his left. 'I've invited Sir John Byron to join us this morning, since we have a joint interest in smoking out the evil that has recently descended on our respective communities. We both require urgent reports as to your progress.'

An ominous silence ensued, as Edward and Francis each hoped that the other would lead the response.

Byron broke the silence. 'Perhaps Mountsorrel could begin by explaining why the witch that I sent him to apprehend was recently reported as having left the place where she was encamped, accompanied by two men who brought a wagon for that purpose.'

'That explains why I could not locate her,' Edward lied as he asked for God's forgiveness. 'She must have received early intelligence of my intention to interrogate her, and took the opportunity to escape before I could do so.'

'Don't presume to treat me like a numbskull!' Byron yelled. 'You were to meet with her on the day that I gave you that instruction. My informant advises me that the wretch in question did indeed have a male visitor on that day — one whose description was remarkably like yours — but that it was several days later when she removed herself with the assistance of two men and a wagon. Explain yourself!'

Edward realised that there was someone in Papplewick who'd been keeping Byron well advised. He would need to spin some credible story to divert suspicion away from himself and preserve Rose from further persecution. First of all, he could attempt to cast doubt on what Byron had been advised.

'If there is someone in the locality who has been keeping watch on the woman in question, and has presumably been reporting on her activities, then why did he not secure her for himself, and bring her to Newstead along with his suspicions?'

'The "he" is a "she",' Byron returned, 'and do not seek to evade my question. Why was she not taken up on the day that you sought her out?'

'I made enquiry, as you instructed,' Edward replied, as inspiration struck, 'and there was a woman with whom I spoke who told me that Magic Mary had moved on from where she had been encamped, and might now be found in the vicinity of Linby, where I spent the remainder of that day searching for her in vain.'

'Describe the woman with whom you spoke, who seems to have misdirected you,' Byron demanded.

Edward was on safer ground by describing Rose accurately. 'She was between forty and fifty years of age, by my estimation, and quite short in height. She was dressed like a field labourer, and had hair that was white, no doubt through constant exposure to the sun. Her manner of speech was surprisingly refined for one of her apparent class, and my overall impression was that she had known better times, perhaps being the widow of a highly regarded servant such as an estate steward.'

'You dolt!' Byron yelled. 'She must have been the very woman you were seeking, since her description matches the one I was given!'

'Had you seen fit to share that description with me, I would then have known who to apprehend,' Edward replied.

He had not expected Byron to take kindly to this response, and he was therefore prepared for the flicker of foam from the sheriff's mouth as he all but screamed, 'You seek to blame *me* for your incompetence?'

'Of course not, Sheriff,' Edward assured him. 'It is simply the case that the woman is clearly quite capable of the deepest deception, and had I been advised of her physical appearance…'

'This same woman may be the one you are both seeking in connection with the recent events at Gallows Hill,' Kniveton suggested, bringing a welcome change to the heated exchange. He looked at Francis. 'What steps have you taken in that regard, Barton?'

'And why was I not advised?' Byron interrupted. 'Gallows Hill lies within *my* jurisdiction, and Mountsorrel might be better employed in tracking her down, if indeed she be the same woman who has brought evil to my estate.'

'We are both making the necessary enquiries,' Francis said, speaking for the first time. 'But so far we have learned nothing to our advantage regarding who might be behind it all.'

'The *Devil* is behind it all!' Kniveton yelled. 'That is obvious, and clearly he has enlisted the assistance of mortals who have bartered their very souls in exchange for the power that Satan can place in their hands. This woman must be found *immediately*, and then hung on the same gallows.'

'Or better still, burned at the stake,' Byron suggested. 'The late Queen Mary found it expeditious to scourge the evil from men's souls by applying a torch to their flesh, or so I am advised by a man who was present at some of those burnings. He is an old man now, but he tells of one who continues to unmask those who do the Devil's work by the simple expedient of pricking their skins.'

'You speak of John Kincaid?' Kniveton asked eagerly. 'I too have heard of his skill in that regard, from my good friend Robert Aldridge, vicar of St Mary's. Perhaps we should enlist his aid in these matters, Sir John, since it would seem that the same woman may lie at the root of each of our problems.'

'There is little point in calling in such a man as Kincaid until we have the woman in our clutches,' Byron reminded him. 'And these two dullards seem unlikely to achieve that, left to their own devices.'

'They have not yet advised us of what steps they have taken,' Kniveton snapped as the prospect of acquiring some credit for the unmasking of a witch seemed to be slipping from his grasp. 'So speak!' he commanded Francis and Edward.

'We've spoken with Thomas Gullen,' Francis explained. 'He's the public hangman, and he occupies a cottage at Gallows Hill, the better to perform his duties. He confirms that strange sounds have been heard at that place nightly. But he hasn't actually witnessed any spectres for himself.'

'Is that all?' Kniveton demanded, red-faced. 'I could produce a dozen people from the town who could tell me the same thing, since it would seem that the ungodly events have become something of a sideshow for the idle and misguided. Have you not attended yourselves, in order to observe those who attend these disgraceful bacchanals?'

'We had it in mind to do so this coming night,' Edward assured him, and both sheriffs nodded their approval.

'It is not before time,' Kniveton conceded. 'Let us hope that the woman who conjures up these dreadful visions cannot do so without being there herself.'

'She may, of course, take the form of her familiar in order to do so,' said Byron, 'so the search will need to be very thorough indeed.'

'It will be,' Francis assured them. 'But you will appreciate that while so much attention is being given to what happens nightly on Gallows Hill, the matters that require my attention elsewhere in the town are being neglected, so if I might be permitted to withdraw and go about my duties?'

'Yes, of course,' Kniveton agreed. 'And I imagine that Sheriff Byron will be similarly disposed towards Bailiff Mountsorrel?'

'On the condition that he loses no time in searching the entire county for the witch from Papplewick, certainly,' Byron conceded, and both men took their leave.

'Where to next, would you suggest?' Francis asked as they walked eagerly away from the house in High Pavement.

'We must prepare ourselves to visit Gallows Hill tonight,' Edward replied gloomily. 'But before that, we must visit the two ladies in Daybrook. Not for the reason that no doubt makes you anxious to return, but to ensure that Mistress Middleham remains unharmed and undetected, and to learn from her who may have been spying on her movements in Papplewick. According to Byron it was a woman, and Rose mentioned a woman who wishes her ill.'

'It sounds as if we shall have another full day, without any appreciation from either of our masters,' Francis complained, but Edward was not in the mood for despondency.

'However, we shall be doing the best we can for the people we are paid to protect, and even though they may not get around to thanking us, we'll have the satisfaction of knowing that. Now, let's see what Meg's prepared for dinner, which you're more than welcome to share with us. However, if you would be so obliging, please make no mention in Elizabeth's hearing of what we are planning for tonight. If, at the same time, you could contrive to convey the impression that our mission to Daybrook may engage us until well after dark, then that will give me a good excuse for arriving home a little ahead of the cock crowing.'

'Need you wonder why I was never attracted to marriage?' Francis said with a smirk.

'You really should dismiss that houseboy of yours, although you are, as ever, welcome to join us at board,' Elizabeth told Francis as the two men appeared in the doorway and began taking off their boots. 'It will, however, be another hour before it's ready, since we did not expect you so early in the day. In truth, we don't normally expect Edward at all, and the pie vendor in Weekday Cross must be bemoaning his loss of custom this week.'

'We need to eat early and well because we have to journey to Arnold, in order to enquire into the activities of a woman suspected of being a witch,' Edward explained. 'I do not anticipate that we shall be back until long after sunset, so tonight it will be my supper that will consist of a pie.'

'Have a care, consorting with witches,' Elizabeth warned him.

He smiled at her reassuringly. 'I said merely that she was *suspected* of being a witch, not that she is one. In fact, we shall be making the trip to confirm that she's come to no harm.'

'Very honourable of you, I'm sure,' Elizabeth replied as she nodded towards the scullery door. 'Now, perhaps you'd care to enquire as to whether your children have come to any harm while attempting to climb that apple tree at the bottom of the garden.'

'Once we've slaked our thirst with some small beer,' Edward replied as he led Francis out into the scullery, where the barrel sat on a wooden bench with mugs laid out in front of it. After inviting Francis to help himself, and to take one out for Margaret, Edward filled two mugs of his own. He then extracted a small handful of Rose Middleham's simple from his tunic pocket and tipped it into one of the mugs as they stepped outside into the pale autumn sunshine.

Margaret reacted to their appearance in her predictable way, racing across the garden and throwing her arms around Francis, almost causing him to spill the two beers in his hand. Edward called for Robert, and in response a small form dropped from a low branch of the apple tree, clutching an apple and grinning as his father handed him the beer mug. He drained the contents of the mug in one swallow, then gave a loud burp that caused both children to giggle.

The two men took their time over dinner, then remounted their horses and headed north towards Daybrook. As they passed Gallows Hill, Francis observed, 'All looks peaceful enough at the moment.'

'Tonight may well be another matter,' said Edward, 'and we must ensure that no-one is aware of our presence. I suggest that we establish ourselves in that shrubbery alongside Gullens's cottage long before the dead of night.'

'Why will we need to hide ourselves from any ghosts, who will surely be aware of our presence anyway?'

'Not from the ghosts,' Edward told him. 'From whoever is producing them.'

As they arrived at Catherine Fellows's orchard, Rose emerged from the cottage with a welcoming smile and wiped her hands on her apron. The two men dismounted and walked towards her, and Edward announced their reason for being there.

'Has anyone been seen approaching the house, or keeping watch on it — other than us, of course?'

'No, why?' Rose asked. Her face registered mild alarm.

'Because it would seem that your every action was being watched in your previous location by the river,' Edward explained. 'Whoever it was reported to Sheriff Byron that you were seen leaving with a wagon, in the company of two men. I hope that we were not followed here the other day, but you must be circumspect in your movements, and perhaps remain within the house.'

'But then I couldn't help Kitty with the apple harvest,' she objected, and that seemed to remind Francis of his true motive for being there.

'I shall obviously be of assistance in that regard,' he assured her. 'So, where is Kitty to be found?'

'In the barn over there,' Rose told him with a knowing smile. 'I'm sure she'll be extremely pleased to welcome you back here.'

Francis disappeared in the direction of the barn, from which, a minute later, a woman could be heard welcoming his appearance with an expression of delight. Edward laughed, then looked back at Rose.

'Kitty has been without a man for too long now, and I hope that your colleague can be of assistance to her in more ways than one,' she told him.

'Believe me, he can,' Edward replied. 'But we must talk more about ensuring your safety. For one thing, you should not be seen out here, in full view of the lane.'

Rose indicated that they should adjourn to the cottage, where she poured them both a mug of recently brewed elderflower wine and asked him how he knew that her departure from Papplewick had been noticed.

'Sheriff Byron seems to have someone spying on your movements,' Edward replied. 'Although if he didn't know where precisely you were to be found, how could that be? There must be someone following on your heels wherever you go, like a hound after a deer, then pouring poison into the sheriff's ear regarding your actions, making your honest and worthy endeavours sound like witchcraft. Who could that be?'

Rose sighed. 'Little mystery there, I'm afraid. I already advised you of my success in ensuring that Kitty married the man to whom she'd lost her heart, but who had been beguiled by our neighbour Agnes Merryweather. If ever a woman used her abilities for ill, it was her. If someone displeased her, they would soon be subjected to stomach cramps or vomiting, and if they threatened to expose what she was doing they would suffer even greater loss. More than one family lost its breadwinner because the woman of that family had slighted Agnes in some way, and God preserve anyone who attempted to cheat her, or report her doings to the authorities. It got so that everyone in Hucknall was mortally afraid of her, but after I employed an art of my own — of which I remain heartily ashamed to this day, but which I did for love of Kitty — Agnes Merryweather seemed to lose her power. All she had left was the fear that others felt towards her. So she began a wicked campaign of untruths regarding my work for good among our neighbours. I had to move to Papplewick, where you found me, but more than once I've spotted her in the trees, spying on my every deed. It was almost certainly she who was keeping watch when we left there, and we can only hope that she was unable to follow us on foot.'

Edward drummed the side of his mug with his fingers, deep in thought. 'Can you tell me precisely where in Hucknall I might find Mistress Merryweather?'

'She had a cottage alongside the mill that used to serve the Manor Hall before it fell into disuse. The cottage was built for the use of the miller — the last one was Agnes's father. After he died there was no more milling, and folk were too frightened of Agnes to insist that she leave the cottage, so she stayed on there, brewing her poisons and casting her evil spells. The mill is at the back of the old Manor Hall.' She hesitated. 'But if you visit Agnes, will she not recognise you as one of those who helped me to come here?'

'She might, but she might not recognise Francis. And even if she does, she will not know him to be the bailiff to the Nottingham sheriff. You're right, though; if she knows that I work for Sheriff Byron, then she'll lose no time in reporting the assistance I gave to you, and then my office would be forfeit.'

'We cannot contemplate that for a single moment,' Rose declared, looking genuinely alarmed. 'You've been so good to me, and I have no way of rewarding you. The least I can do is to ensure that you do not lose by it.'

Edward took her hand and squeezed it gently. 'In truth, you have already performed a great service for me. The simple that you gave me for my son Robert has worked wonders, and he now smiles, eats, and has even begun to talk, although he is still a little lacking in that, given his late start. So some more of that simple would be a more than adequate reward.'

'That will be no trouble at all,' Rose assured him as she got to her feet and walked to the bench against the rear wall of the humble cottage, on which she'd installed her mortar and pestle. 'But remember what I said about not exceeding the dose. And once the boy's humour has become fixed as you would wish, you must cease giving him the simple, lest an excess of it causes him harm of a different order. Now, will you and Francis stay and partake of some of the newly baked bread that you can smell in the oven out there? I also made some goats' cheese the day after I arrived here. It should still be fresh, and although it is perhaps too late for dinner and too early for supper, you men must be hungry, and you have to journey back to Nottingham. By the time you reach your homes it will be fully dark and you will be hungry.'

'As it transpires,' said Edward, 'we have other duties that will occupy us well into the hours of darkness, so a little sustenance now would be very welcome. Shall we invite Francis and Kitty to join us?'

Rose moved to the cottage door and called Kitty's name loudly. There was a muffled response from the direction of the barn, from which emerged, a short while later, a red-faced Kitty adjusting her bodice and a grinning Francis brushing straw from his hose and boots.

As the bailiffs guided their horses back down the lane in the fading light two hours later, Francis could barely contain his delight. 'I never imagined that sorting apples could be so pleasurable,' he declared. 'I shall return here at the first opportunity.'

'You will have occasion enough to fondle ripe fruit when all this is over,' Edward admonished him. 'And you would oblige me greatly if this time you could contrive to commit to matrimony with the lady. But for the time being we must direct our thoughts to less pleasant matters.'

'I had almost forgotten,' Francis mumbled resignedly.

'Fortunately, I had not,' Edward replied. 'You must turn your attention from investigating bodices to enquiring into witchcraft and visitations from the dead.'

7

Edward looked up mournfully at the thick clouds obscuring the moon and heard another soft curse from Francis, who was kneeling beside him. They were cold, hungry, uncomfortable and bored, and the damp was eating into their hose as they knelt in the leaf litter inside the bushes that lined the track running past Thomas Gullen's cottage. It was so dark that they could not even make out the shadow of the gallows frame that they knew was located only feet away from them, and now it was starting to drizzle.

'How much bloody longer are we going to crouch here like town burglars, waiting for something that may not happen?' Francis demanded.

Edward shushed him before whispering back hoarsely, 'It'll happen, believe me — the audience is too large for it not to. It's just a matter of time.'

The audience to which he referred could be heard rather than seen. All around them they could make out furtive whispers, the murmur of apprehensive conversation and the occasional nervous giggle. Edward leaned forward slightly in a futile effort to detect any movement that might indicate the presence of a group of players setting up for a new performance, then settled back on his rapidly dampening knees with a frustrated sigh. Then, just as he was beginning to give way to his own worry that they were wasting their time, it began.

A whirring scream rent the stillness as a red flame shot into the air from somewhere within the copse of trees through which they had chased the woman at the hanging, followed by another travelling in the opposite direction. A third shot up vertically.

'Squibs,' Edward told Francis. 'The stock-in-trade of any group of strolling players.'

What followed next was less easily written off as a stage effect. There was a mighty roar of devilish laughter, followed by a booming voice that seemed to emanate from the bowels of the earth.

'The witch's curse has once more called us back to the land of the living,' the voice announced. 'We who were hanged here without mercy will take our revenge on those who mocked our death agonies! Behold our images and tremble!'

A loud rumbling like distant thunder preceded a blinding flash, and from the earth rose a ghostly skull with flickering red eyes that hovered eight feet or so above the ground between the trees. There was a collective gasp from the audience as more streamers of light flashed across their line of vision. A bellow of sepulchral laughter was followed by another dire warning.

'Those of you here for mere entertainment have this night forfeited your souls to the Prince of Darkness! Go back to your hovels knowing that mankind is doomed to be dragged into the pit of Hell for its wickedness in persecuting the Daughters of Darkness who serve the real Lord of the Elements. This land shall soon be plunged into eternal darkness, under the mantle of which each of you shall be dragged into the tortures that await you. Go, and live in fear until the Prince of Hades arrives to claim your souls!'

Shrieks and sobs could be heard as the gathered crowd rapidly dispersed in confusion and terror, tripping over each other in the darkness as they scrambled for their very lives. Edward and Francis remained where they were until there was no more sound, and the flaming skull slowly sank out of sight. Francis, breathing heavily, asked, 'Did you ever see strolling players pull off a performance like that, Edward, or has the witch's curse taken effect?'

'It had the desired effect all right,' Edward confirmed, 'but not in the manner that you imply. I should like to see a return performance when the moon is brighter.'

'Some people are easily entertained,' Francis grumbled. 'May we go now? My knees feel like winter cabbages, and I would prefer the comfort of my own bed.'

Edward chuckled. 'That display had *one* remarkable outcome anyway, if you seek your own bed rather than someone else's.'

Francis had more discomfort awaiting him the following morning, when he entered his chamber under the Guildhall to find Sheriff George Stokely awaiting him. Although Stokely held his shrieval office jointly with William Kniveton, he was far less likely to interfere with the work of his bailiff and the constables that he had at his command, being content merely to bask in the prestige of his title and use it to further both his business and his political ambitions. His presence in Francis's office so early in the day was not a matter for rejoicing on Francis's part.

'I was wondering if I still had a bailiff,' Stokely announced sardonically, 'given the number of complaints I have received regarding the state of the lower town. It seems that the alehouses have taken to serving liquor around the clock, thereby generating hordes of inebriates who foul the streets with their vomit, piss and other abominations, while prostitutes lift their skirts with wild abandon even where their despicable trade may be witnessed by honest citizens as they look on from their windows.'

'Honest citizens who do not possess shutters might at least ensure that they are not standing by their windows in order to witness such ribaldry,' Francis could not resist arguing back. He instantly regretted it as Stokely banged his fist down heavily on the rickety desk.

'This is no time for such levity, Barton! Why are your constables not cracking heads in order to empty the alehouses, and why are there currently no prostitutes awaiting judgement before the magistrates?'

'In truth, Sheriff,' replied Francis, 'my constables have been fully engaged in business further north of here, at the insistence of Sheriff Kniveton.'

'I suspected as much!' Stokely grimaced. 'I allow you as much freedom as I dare to conduct your office as you see fit, and you repay me by leaping to attention whenever Kniveton demands that you engage in futile pursuits such as the unmasking of so-called witches. While you do so, the noble town of Nottingham begins to resemble that shambles along the south bank of the Thames, with its stews, theatres and bear pits.'

'I have no familiarity with London, Sheriff,' Francis replied, 'and I am bound to obey an order from a sheriff — whoever that may be.'

'You have been commanded to watch for so-called manifestations of the Devil at Gallows Hill, have you not?'

'Indeed, and last night we obtained clear evidence of such.'

'Who is "we", might I ask?' Stokely demanded.

Francis recounted in detail the events of the previous night, resulting in a snort of dismissal from Stokely.

'It was a mistake to appoint that secret Papist Kniveton to such an important office,' he complained. 'He sees angels on rooftops, devils in basements, and the handiwork of the saints in every churchyard. He and that blasphemer Aldridge should be run out of town, and I shall lose no time in reporting to London on how matters have been allowed to degenerate in recent months, under their influence. There are darker forces at work here than toothless old hags with familiars sucking at their nipples, mark my words. My good friend Sir John Popham shall hear of this without delay!'

Reference to the Chief Justice of England caused Francis to reconsider his earlier casual response. It was one thing to justify the dereliction of normal duties on the grounds that he was merely obeying the order of one of his two employers, but another thing altogether to be regarded as one who still believed in all the unfathomable mysteries championed by the outlawed Church of Rome. Devils, curses, witchcraft, evil spells and saintly intervention for the welfare of souls belonged in a dangerous past, and although Her Majesty was tolerant, to a degree, of the religious beliefs of her subjects, she was rumoured to be very unforgiving when those beliefs threatened the very fabric of her nation, and the strength of her grip on the Church.

'What do you desire of me, Sheriff?' he asked meekly, and was less than reassured as Stokely's expression darkened.

'That you perform your duties, you credulous oaf!' Stokely replied tetchily. 'Cease giving credence to all this Popish gibberish regarding witches, curses and the manifestation of the spirits of the dead and get back to clearing the streets of riff-raff. I want to hear no more of fornication in doorways, drunken sops lying in the laneways, and piles of human waste befouling our thoroughfares. I shall be watching and awaiting results, and bear in mind that to me falls the solemn duty of appointing a bailiff to support the work of my office!'

With that he stormed out, leaving Francis in little doubt that he would need to choose his time carefully before taking leave in order to pick apples.

'Regard yourself as fortunate that you only have one sheriff to whom you're answerable,' Francis grumbled as he and Edward stood in the queue for the pie vendor's stall in Weekday Cross. 'Not only that,' Francis added ruefully, 'but he's mercifully half a day's ride north of here.'

'That didn't stop him coming into town two days ago,' Edward replied, 'and am I to regard myself as fortunate that my movements at dinner time are so predictable that you can always find me at the pie stall? I take it that this encounter is not accidental?'

'Indeed it is not,' Francis confirmed. 'I'm here about Sheriff Stokely.'

'That makes a change,' said Edward as he reached the front of the queue and handed over his penny in exchange for a mutton pie. 'You normally fulminate against Kniveton. What's brought this on?'

'Stokely's threatening to write to London and have someone sent up here to deal with our difficulty on Gallows Hill.'

'All the better,' Edward observed as they walked towards the front doors of the Guildhall. 'It will relieve us of the need to spend another night on our knees in wet leaves.'

'But he's also complaining that I've been neglecting my duties within the town,' Francis grumbled. 'It's not my fault if one employer gives me an instruction that the other seeks to elevate into a dereliction of duty. I'll have to spend every night from now on ensuring that the streets are clear of undesirables, and that the alehouses close before midnight.'

'That will leave you free during the day, will it not?' Edward asked as they passed through the front hall of Francis's place of employment and headed down the back stairs towards his chamber.

'This is hardly the time for jests,' Francis griped, then he took a closer look at the serious expression on Edward's face. 'Except that wasn't a jest, was it? Please tell me that my days will be free to pick apples?'

'I'm not your employer,' Edward reminded him. 'But I *do* require a favour from you, in return for which I'll undertake to supervise your constables as they set about cleansing the night-time streets.'

'What do you have in mind?' Francis asked warily as they reached his chamber and took a seat.

'I wish you to journey north to a village called Linby, and seek out a woman called Agnes Merryweather.'

'That doesn't sound too onerous,' said Francis. 'What information do you seek from her?'

'None, at present, but I wish you to note her movements, enquire subtly regarding her habits, and generally learn all you can about the woman.'

'Why? And why can you not undertake such a simple task yourself?'

'I believe that she may have been keeping watch on Rose Middleham during her days in Papplewick. I also suspect that she was watching when you and I assisted Rose to move to Daybrook, which is why I do not wish to make those enquiries myself. As the county bailiff I'm too well known around those parts, and may even have been seen with the wagon at Papplewick. You, on the other hand, are less well known.'

'But I also accompanied that cart,' Francis pointed out. 'Will I not also be recognised if I come across her?'

'That's why you must simply make enquiry regarding her movements, her activities and so on,' said Edward. 'You're less likely to be remembered than me, since you're normally town-based. If it's any consolation, you can call in at Daybrook on your way back and sample whatever fruit may be on offer.'

'You know me too well,' Francis said, grinning appreciatively. 'You are also very persuasive, but I'll hold you to your promise to lead my men in a clean-up of the streets — beginning tonight.'

'Really, it's not good enough!' Elizabeth complained as Edward gave his reason for requiring an early supper. 'You were out all last night, and now you tell me that you've undertaken to do Francis's job, risking your own neck brawling with local ruffians. And all *this* at a time when the Devil's loose among us. Do you not care to stay home and protect those closest to your heart?'

Edward sighed. 'I have no choice, I'm afraid. Francis will be engaged with important matters in the county, and the least I can do is relieve him of some of his duties. Sheriff Stokely is becoming very threatening towards him regarding the state that the lower town has got into while we've been investigating other incidents.'

'Such as the goings-on at Gallows Hill?' Elizabeth demanded suspiciously. 'Is *that* where you were when you crawled in here at God knows when last night? And Meg tells me that your hose were soaking wet when you left them for her to wash. Were you crawling through the undergrowth, or did you have an accident?'

'Mamma tell Daddy off!' Robert said, giggling loudly.

'It may have been a mistake encouraging you to talk!' Edward muttered as he headed upstairs to dress for what promised to be a challenging night.

It turned out to be all that Edward had dreaded, and more. By the next morning, he and three constables had filled the Guildhall cells with robbers, drunks, street prostitutes and one alehouse landlord who'd taken a swing at Edward when he'd insisted that the Three Tuns be closed down for the night. The man now had a broken nose to add to his night's misfortunes, while Edward was sporting a very swollen eye socket.

But the message had been delivered loudly and clearly, and when Francis appeared for duty at the start of a new working day, he smiled with appreciation at the list of those apprehended, and began sorting them according to categories of offence.

'Presumably the prostitutes are for the magistrates,' he said with a chuckle, 'but what about Ned Paulson? Does punching a bailiff not earn you an appearance at the Quarter Sessions?'

'He's already acquired a broken nose,' Edward said with a smirk, 'so leave him to the magistrates, with a recommendation that he be replaced as landlord by someone with a more healthy respect for authority. But there's one man down in the cells that you might want to look at more carefully — name of Baggot. Unless he can provide a more satisfactory explanation for his possession of the silver altar chalice we found stuffed up his undershirt, perhaps let the Quarter Sessions decide his sentence for robbing St Mary's.'

'You've done very well,' Francis congratulated Edward, 'but good luck in explaining that shiner to Elizabeth.'

'At least it'll support my story that I was brawling in town, which she regards as infinitely preferable to perjuring my soul on Gallows Hill. And I haven't forgotten that we need to go back for another performance on a night when the moon is full.'

'You begin to sound as if you actually believe what you previously dismissed as superstitious fiddle-faddle,' Francis commented. 'Aren't witches supposed to mount their broomsticks at the full moon?'

'No idea,' Edward replied. 'But *you* promised to mount your horse and journey to Linby in search of Agnes Merryweather, remember?'

'I am hardly likely to forget,' Francis said with a grin, 'when I have fruit to sample on the way back.'

Francis was back in Daybrook much earlier than he'd anticipated, due largely to the reason for his swift departure from Linby. As promised, he'd entered the small village before midday, and he found the abandoned mill behind the equally abandoned old Manor Hall without any difficulty. It had then been a simple matter of finding someone who could advise him regarding the current location, lifestyle, habits and disposition of Agnes Merryweather. His first — and, as it transpired, his only — enquiry was made of a youth of around sixteen years of age lounging against a rotting gate post at the start of the weed-infested former path to the Manor Hall.

The youth took time to clear his mouth of the portion of apple that he'd been chewing, before asking, 'Why d'you wanna know?'

'That's my business,' Francis replied.

The youth smirked. 'Got a dose of the pox, have you? Agnes can fix that for you, but if you're after getting one, then Alice Colley's the one you needs to go with. She's to be found in that cottage on the other side of the bridge that you just passed over. Tell her that Billy Tranter sent you and it'll only cost you fourpence.'

'I'm more interested in Agnes Merryweather.'

'Trust me, you'd do much better with Alice. So mebbe you *have* got a dose of the pox after all. Agnes can cure that, along with lots of other stuff.'

'Does she travel from place to place?' Francis asked. 'Or does she bide all her time in that old mill cottage?'

'What's it to you?' the youth demanded. 'She's in there at the moment, anyroad, so best get up there afore she moves on for the day.'

'Does she go abroad every day?' Francis persisted, and this time the youth's eyes narrowed in suspicion.

'You seem mighty interested in learning about her movements, for a bloke that simply wants summat to cure the pox.'

'I don't have the pox,' Francis insisted.

'What is it, then?' the youth demanded. 'Boils on the arse? Smelly farts?'

'My business with her is my *own* business,' Francis replied coolly. 'But if you can tell me more about Agnes Merryweather, there may be a few pence in it for you.'

'She in trouble again?' the youth demanded.

Francis seized on the point. 'How do you mean *again*?' he asked, just as the youth began to slink away.

'I've said enough already — sling your hook,' he muttered as he walked smartly back towards the village.

A frustrated Francis decided to move closer to the mill cottage in the hope of catching sight of the lady after whom he'd been enquiring. He got as close as he dared, but there was no sign of movement, so he reluctantly turned his horse's head and walked him gently down to the track that led in and out of the village, where a group of surly men were waiting for him.

'You the lard-arse what's been enquiring about our Agnes?' one of them demanded.

Francis sat higher in the saddle to emphasise his height advantage as he replied, haughtily, 'Why do you wish to know?'

''Cos we don't take kindly to strangers sticking their noses where they don't belong,' the man replied as he nodded to one of his companions, who took hold of the bridle of Francis's mount to prevent him riding off.

'Sometimes we cut them noses off,' another man growled.

'You should know that I'm the bailiff to the Sheriff of Nottingham,' Francis asserted with more confidence than he felt.

The first man greeted this information by spitting on the ground. 'But this ain't Nottingham, so you've no rightful business here, have you?'

'That's for me to know,' Francis defied him, 'and if you're friends of Agnes Merryweather's, then perhaps you'd be good enough to advise me why you think it necessary to protect her in this manner.'

'None of your business,' the first man retorted, 'so piss off now, while your horse has still got four legs.'

Two of the men produced wicked-looking scythe blades from under their cloaks, and Francis formed the hasty conclusion that his enquiries had been completed for the day. He wrenched hard on the horse's bridle, ripping it from the loosened grip of the man who'd been holding it, then dug his boots into the animal's sides, making it leap forward and forcing two of the men to jump hastily to one side for their own safety. As he thundered back down the road to the south, he heard one of them yell after him, 'Come back here again and you're dead!'

8

Francis dismounted in the yard adjacent to Rose's cottage in Daybrook and looked hopefully across at the apple barn in anticipation of Kitty appearing at the door with her welcoming smile. But the barn doors were barred.

He looked back towards the cottage door in time to see Rose peering out at him with a scowl of determination. 'Hello!' he called out cheerfully. 'Am I still welcome here?'

'Of course you are,' Rose replied sheepishly as she opened the door wider, to reveal that she had a large club in her hand. Kitty's face appeared behind her, then she slipped past her sister to embrace Francis warmly.

'Sorry about that,' she murmured as she offered her face up for a kiss, 'but we can't be too careful.'

'Careful of what?' Francis asked.

Rose invited him inside and poured him a mug of elderberry wine before explaining. 'We've been robbed. Sometime last night, it must have been. Ten barrels of our best apples. Whoever it was must have had a wagon to carry them off in, but we never heard a thing. Not even our dog, Toby — he slept through it all, so they must have been as silent as the grave.'

'That's bad news,' Francis commiserated. 'Have you reported the theft?'

Rose nodded with a grimace. 'Yes, for all the use *that* was. The local constable just told us that it's happening all over the district, and there's not a lot I can do about it, so pardon us if we just lost any faith we might have had in the maintenance of the law around these parts.'

'No need to apologise to me,' said Francis, 'since I'm only responsible for upholding the Queen's Peace in the town. But I'll pass on your complaint to Edward, who as you know is the county bailiff.'

'Could you remain with us overnight?' Kitty asked hopefully. 'We still have another four barrels that they obviously couldn't carry off with them the first time. With you here, they may think twice about coming back.'

'I certainly can if it's necessary to keep you safe,' Francis agreed, 'but do you have a spare room?'

There was a brief embarrassed silence, before Kitty replied, 'No, but I'd already decided where you might lay your head, and Rose is a heavy sleeper. In fact, we both are, which is no doubt how they got away with it.'

'Then that's decided,' Francis said with a grin of anticipation. 'But wouldn't it be better if I slept in the barn?'

'For catching thieves, probably,' Rose replied. 'But I think that Kitty would much prefer her protector closer to hand, so to speak. Now, would you like an early supper?'

An hour later as they sat across from each other on either side of a splendid platter of bread, cheeses, cold meats and freshly boiled eggs, Rose looked hard at Francis and remarked, 'You put yourself in great danger today.'

Francis shrugged and managed a smile. 'Come now, your cooking's not *that* bad.'

'That's not what I meant, and you know it,' Rose said. 'You went to Linby, didn't you?'

'How could you possibly know that?' Francis demanded.

'I have this gift, as you know,' Rose reminded him. 'You must be careful — those ruffians do Agnes Merryweather's bidding in the hope of benefitting from her supposed power. A power she no longer has, but they aren't to know that.'

'You're right, of course,' Francis conceded. 'Edward asked me to travel to Linby to find out what I could about Agnes, since she may still be a threat to you. In fact, without wishing to frighten you unduly, it's his belief that Agnes may have been spying on you when you left Papplewick, and reported back to Sheriff Byron. As you know, she's already decried you as the witch responsible for certain portentous events on his estate that he puts down to witchcraft.'

'Such nonsense!' Rose replied. 'As I already advised Edward, all those recent happenings on the Newstead estate have simple explanations that have nothing to do with witchcraft.'

'I'm sure you're right,' Francis agreed, 'but Byron has clearly been persuaded otherwise, no doubt by Agnes. You must have really angered her in the past, for her to still be seeking her revenge.'

'Did Edward not tell you?' Kitty intervened. 'I was all set to marry my late husband Thomas Fellows, when Agnes cast some sort of charm over him, and he seemed to lose all affection for me.'

'Agnes *did* have special powers in those days,' Rose confirmed, 'but on that occasion I cursed her myself, God forgive me, and the spell she'd exercised over Thomas fell away, and Kitty was able to reclaim him. Agnes never forgave me for that, and I think she blames me for the loss of her other powers, although in truth, as I said, it was her own wickedness that was her downfall.'

'But from what you tell me,' Francis said, 'she is still believed by others to possess the powers she once had, which is why they are so protective of her?'

'Yes,' said Rose, 'and they're a murderous lot, believe me. They live outside the law most of the time, thieving and threatening honest folk in the belief that Agnes somehow has them under her protective cloak, when if the truth be known it's just because folk are so fearful of them. They're well known all the way to Mansfield, and they just do what they like. They are probably responsible for stealing our apples.'

'Edward shall hear of all this,' Francis promised as he sat back with a contented sigh from the feast that he'd consumed. 'And now I think I'll just take a turn around the barn, if only to make sure that it's secure.'

As he came round the rear of the apple barn in the failing light he found Kitty waiting for him, slightly flushed in the face. She wrapped her arms around him and kissed him warmly on the lips.

'I hope you don't think me too forward, offering to let you share my chamber. Rose really *is* a heavy sleeper.'

'All to the good,' Francis replied, 'since we're likely to make a certain amount of noise before we finally fall asleep. And might I suggest that we have an early night?'

'I was hoping you'd suggest that,' she said, looking up at him coyly. 'Let's see just how strong the arm of the law is around these parts, shall we?'

'I filled the cells again,' Edward told him testily, as Francis arrived back at the Guildhall shortly before noon the following day. 'But you can take over again tonight. Elizabeth's threatening to take the children down to Ashby to live with their grandparents if I don't go home to my own bed tonight. Where have you been?'

'Not in my own bed, certainly,' Francis replied cheerfully, as he recalled the night of passion during which neither he nor Kitty had slept, heavily or otherwise. 'But I have news to impart from your jurisdiction.'

'I was about to purchase a pie,' Edward told him, 'since the atmosphere around my breakfast table was not conducive to a hearty appetite. Walk with me, and perhaps purchase a pie of your own. While you're about it, you can purchase one for me.'

They sat on the bench just inside St Mary's churchyard, surveying the old gravestones and eating their dinner. 'I take it from the grin on your face, and the eagerness with which you're renewing your energy courtesy of a hot mutton pie, that you had a most enjoyable night in a certain cottage adjoining an orchard in Daybrook,' Edward commented sourly.

'I most certainly did,' Francis replied as he wiped mutton grease from his chin. 'But I have news to impart other than the warmth of the welcome I received from Mistress Catherine. For one thing, I was unable to locate Agnes Merryweather, and when I began asking locally regarding her habits and character, I was ordered out of Linby by a bunch of thugs. Had I been accompanied by constables I might have made a stand, but in the circumstances I beat a hasty retreat and called in at Daybrook on my way back here, as I had intended. But then I learned that the sisters had been robbed the previous night — ten barrels of their best apples — and that the local constable had been cool in his response when they reported it.'

Edward nodded. 'That would be Will Draycott, the Arnold Constable,' he told Francis. 'He's an idlemonger at the best of times, and it's not the first complaint I've received regarding his unwillingness to perform his duties. Have there been any other thefts, did they say?'

'Apparently the constable told them that there have been some other incidents in the district. Whoever was responsible for stealing the apples seems to have been well organised. They made no sound — not even alerting the dog to their presence — and they must have had the use of a cart of some sort.'

'I'll go up to Hucknall this afternoon,' said Edward, 'and ask if any crop thefts have been reported there; if the constable reports similar complaints, we might manage to get a force of local men together to catch them at it.'

'If that's the case, then the least I can do is lend you some of my constables to assist,' Francis offered. 'And I'll even undertake to go with you.'

Edward raised an eyebrow. 'Hoping for another tryst in Daybrook?'

'If it's anything like the one last night, most certainly.'

'I was about to send word down to you,' Robert Gledhill, the Hucknall constable, told Edward, who had made enquiry regarding recent thefts of autumn crops. 'There was a bunch of them at it a couple of years back, if you recall, but we soon had them put away. Now it seems like it's started again. There have been complaints from Eastwood, Kimberley and Mansfield, and now you tell me they've been down to Daybrook as well. No doubt if we ask in Woodthorpe we'll get the same story.'

'Any idea who might be behind it?' Edward asked.

Gledhill scratched his stubbly chin. 'There's a bad bunch out Linby way, always into something or other, but you'll need quite a few constables to take them on, 'cos they always cuts up rough.'

'The thieves must have a market for what they steal. Have you heard of anyone new around the local markets, selling produce? People who don't have farms or orchards of their own?'

'No, but I could always make enquiry,' Gledhill offered. 'The biggest market round here is Mansfield, as you probably know for yourself. It's on every Saturday, and I usually go down there in case there are any fights or other disorder, like stealing from stalls. Do you want me to keep a special lookout for any new folks, bearing in mind that I knows most of the regular traders?'

'Better than that, Robert — take me round with you next Saturday,' Edward suggested. 'I'll bring some extra men with me, and we'll see if we can't catch them red-handed, so to speak.'

The following Saturday Edward and Francis walked slowly up and down the crowded lanes of eager purchasers between the dozens of stalls that had been erected for the Mansfield market. Given the season, there were many local traders looking to sell their fresh crops, so the two bailiffs needed to take their time and look carefully for anyone posing as a regular trader who didn't quite look like a farmer. A contingent of constables had been drafted in from neighbouring communities, and they were awaiting a signal from Edward to move in if they found the malefactors they were looking for. Francis suddenly stopped and grabbed Edward's arm.

'Up there on the left — the stall with all the apples piled high! The man standing behind it is the one who ordered me out of Linby when I went looking for Agnes Merryweather. The others grouped round him look familiar, too.'

'You're certain?' Edward asked.

Francis spat on the earth in front of his boots. 'You don't easily forget someone armed with a scythe who's threatening to cut your nose off. Go and get the men!'

The melee that followed was bloody and hard-fought, and it effectively cleared the market of honest folk who were there for their next week's supplies, and not to witness a mass brawl involving a dozen men armed with clubs and staves, and — in several cases — wicked-looking scythe blades. But eventually

Edward and his team had five men securely trussed by their ankles and wrists lying in the bottom of a wagon headed for Mansfield in the early afternoon sun.

9

'This goes nicely with the black eye you came home with three nights ago,' Elizabeth observed unsympathetically as she bathed the deep gash on Edward's forehead while the children looked on in fascinated horror. 'And stop wriggling about,' she added as Edward flinched. 'Perhaps I'll marry a physician next time — then he can heal his own wounds. How did you get this one, anyway?'

'In Mansfield market, rounding up a bunch of fruit thieves who'd raided the orchard owned by Francis's latest widow,' Edward replied. 'If it's any consolation, the one who did it will probably need a bone-setter for his arm.'

'It's of no consolation whatsoever,' Elizabeth muttered as she dipped the cloth back into the bowl, 'but hopefully it means that you'll be home again tonight.'

'Ask him,' Edward replied, as Francis breezed through the door. He was almost bowled over as an eager Margaret threw herself at him with cries of welcome.

'Ask me what?' Francis asked as he disentangled himself.

'Whether or not I'll be home tonight.'

'That's clearly a matter for you, since we seem to have collected enough malefactors to satisfy Sheriff Stokely for the time being. That's partly why I'm here, actually — the Guildhall cells are full, and I was going to enquire whether or not you had some spare room in yours under the Shire Hall, but then I received word from your turnkey that you're about to become overloaded yourself. It seems that the men we arrested in Mansfield are being transferred here later today ahead of your Michaelmas Quarter Sessions. I thought I'd better warn you, because you'll need to check them off the list that we made in Mansfield.'

'Do you by any chance know of any wealthy physicians?' Elizabeth asked.

A look of concern crossed Francis's face. 'Why? Is that head wound worse than it looks?'

'My reason for asking is that I was thinking of marrying one when you succeed in killing my current husband. Edward tells me that you both went to Mansfield market because your latest widow had her apples stolen.'

Edward suppressed a chortle. 'They were already well handled, thanks to Francis.'

'I wasn't aware that my affairs of the heart were a matter of general discussion across the road from my dwelling,' Francis replied starchily, 'and I only came in to warn Edward that he'll need to report to the Shire Hall. But since I'm here, is there any risk of breakfast?'

'Do us all a favour and marry this latest one,' Elizabeth replied as she called into the scullery for Meg to bring some bread and cheese.

'You're about as popular this morning as I am, Francis,' Edward observed as he gingerly pressed his fingers to his forehead. 'And I hope that the Widow Fellows is duly grateful for the effort we expended on her behalf.'

'I'll let you know in due course,' Francis promised as he held out his arms for another cuddle from Margaret. 'In the meantime, I'm taking your daughter to breakfast.'

An hour later Edward was frowning at the list presented to him by Robert Gledhill, who'd accompanied his prisoners in the cart from Mansfield, and was waiting for Edward to receipt the list so that he could begin the two-hour ride home, along with the two outlying village constables who'd accompanied him.

'There are only four on this list,' Edward pointed out, 'but we apprehended five men. What happened to the fifth?'

'Edwin Struthers — the one who took a scythe to your head,' Gledhill told him. 'Sheriff Byron had him released without charge.'

'Because I broke his arm?' asked Edward.

Gledhill shrugged. 'The sheriff didn't give a reason. And his arm wasn't broken, by the way — just badly sprained.'

'The rest are all charged with grand theft, as indeed they should be,' Edward reminded Gledhill, 'and at the very least they are at risk of the pillory, if not a long period in the House of Correction. For one of them to have been released without charge is a serious matter, particularly if the sheriff had no information regarding the strength of the case against him. Did Sheriff Byron seek such information from you before ordering the man's release?'

'No, sir,' Gledhill replied. 'But Struthers were the worst of them. He seems to be the leader of those that run Linby like they own it, and it may be that the sheriff wanted to keep on his right side. But I *can* tell you that Struthers got his fancy woman to take a message up to Newstead the same night he was arrested, and that he was released the following afternoon.'

'Curious,' Edward observed out loud. 'I think I may have to journey to Newstead for myself, in order to seek an answer to this mystery.'

Three hours later, Edward was being kept waiting in a side chamber by the Newstead steward. 'The master has an important visitor, sir,' the steward told him, 'but I'll remind him that you're still here.'

Edward was on the point of leaving when the adjoining door to the great hall was flung open and Byron appeared with a scowl.

'In here, Mountsorrel,' the sheriff announced.

As Edward passed through the opening, he became aware of the visitor to whom the steward had referred earlier. He was a bony little man with eyes like sharp black stones, and he sported a neatly trimmed black beard. His clothes were also black, and his overall appearance was that of a bird of prey waiting for a small furry creature to break cover from the undergrowth.

'This gentleman is John Kincaid, from the Scottish Court,' Byron told him.

Edward's heart sank as he recognised the name. 'The man who searches out witches?' he asked, and Kincaid inclined his head slightly in acknowledgement.

'Which is more than *you* have managed to achieve,' Byron responded accusingly, reclaiming his seat by the fire, and leaving Edward standing before them both. 'Or at least, it would seem that you *did* find one, but elected to keep her hidden from me. You recall my instruction to you to locate the woman called Magic Mary?'

'I do, sir,' Edward conceded.

'And it would seem that you did indeed locate her, then took it upon yourself to spirit her away to a place of hiding. Where precisely might that be?'

'I'm not entirely sure that...' Edward began, only to be drowned out by a bellow from Byron.

'*Silence*! You were instructed to bring her to me for a burning, were you not?'

'Yes, sir.'

'Then why did you not do so? And what have you done with her?'

'What has led to your suspicion that I am hiding her away?' Edward asked, playing for time, and conscious of the penetrating stare from Kincaid.

'I have my sources,' Byron replied enigmatically. 'But suffice it to say that you and another man were seen helping her to transfer her possessions onto a wagon, which was then driven south.'

Suddenly the penny dropped, and Edward no longer needed to enquire as to why Edwin Struthers had been released without charge. He'd bought his freedom by advising Byron of what he or Agnes must have witnessed when watching Edward and Francis removing Rose from Papplewick. By capturing those responsible for stealing her sister's apples, they'd unwittingly put Rose in even worse danger.

'So where *is* she?' Byron demanded.

'Held in secure custody in Nottingham,' Edward lied.

'Why there, and not here?' Byron demanded, red-faced.

'Because if she indeed be a witch, and if she has evil designs on yourself and your estate, then I would be placing you in great danger by bringing her here. Far better that she be held in a secure cell in the town, watched over night and day by gaolers who are made of sterner stuff than to be dissuaded from their sworn duty by simple parlour tricks. And for another reason,' he persevered, 'I am not persuaded that she *is* indeed a witch.'

'And who are you to be making such assessments?' Byron challenged him. 'These are best conducted by those with experience in such matters, such as Master Kincaid here. He has unmasked many such devils, masquerading as harmless old ladies. He is too modest to extol his own achievements in this regard, so I will do it for him, with his leave.'

Kincaid nodded, and Byron continued.

'Master Kincaid preserved the soul of His Majesty King James from a devilish pestilence that had swept through his land in Scotland. Because England seems to have become the next roosting place of Satan and his acolytes, he has been summoned south to rid the land of a similar abomination, and has already enjoyed considerable success, first in the area of Newcastle, to the north of here, and latterly in Chelmsford, in Essex. He has an infallible gift for unmasking witches in all their wickedness.'

'He pricks their skin?' Edward offered.

'How do you know of this?' Byron demanded, and Edward bowed his head slightly as he explained that he'd learned it from Sheriff Kniveton.

'The pricking test has never been known to fail,' said Byron, 'and you will bring the witch known as Magic Mary back here immediately for it to be administered to her.'

'Why here?' Edward asked. 'If she is found to be a witch, then she will be put to death, will she not? Burned or hanged.'

Kincaid spoke for the first time. 'We burn witches in Scotland.'

'And those that you exposed here in England?'

'They were hanged. On the same day that they were exposed.'

'Either way, this woman faces death if proved to be a witch,' Edward persisted. 'Since those charged with murder or robbery are tried in public before their guilt is established, why should it not be the same for those accused of witchcraft?'

'That is not how these matters are conducted in Scotland,' Kincaid told him coldly.

'I care not how things are done in Scotland, Master Kincaid!' Edward responded angrily. 'I care only that justice be carried out here in England in the manner that it has been conducted for centuries — following a public trial, with witnesses and such other items of proof as may exist.'

Kincaid looked at Byron with a challenge in his eyes, but the sheriff could see that Edward was likely to create a good deal of trouble if the due processes of the law were not observed.

'Very well, Mountsorrel,' he conceded. 'You will present this woman inside the Shire Hall in seven days' time, when Master Kincaid will subject her to the test in full public view. Now leave us.'

Edward rode away in a quandary. He grappled with a desperate urge to ride hard to Daybrook and persuade Rose to flee the district, adopt a different name and lose herself where no-one would ever suspect who she was. But even by riding to her new home he risked being followed, and having Rose taken back to Newstead to be burned at the stake. He had managed to persuade Byron that she was in safe custody in the town. This would buy her seven days in which to cover a fair distance, and he owed her that at least for the miraculous change she had wrought in his young son. But he was a sworn officer of the law, and to facilitate Rose's escape would not only be a betrayal of his office, but would almost certainly result in his dismissal. Quite apart from the consequences for the welfare of his own family, and the public disgrace, he would no longer be in a position to assist Rose — assuming that he could anyway.

Carefully avoiding Daybrook by taking the more direct road by way of Bestwood, Edward arrived home an hour after sunset. He hitched his horse outside Francis's house and hammered on the front door.

His knock was answered by Francis's houseboy, Ralph, who opened the door wider when Edward asked whether Francis was home. Edward found him seated by an open fire, ale mug in hand, and minus his boots, which lay on the rushes in front of him as he offered his hosed feet to the warmth.

'Francis,' Edward told him breathlessly, 'you need to ride hard to Daybrook and tell Rose to lose herself somewhere safe, and preferably a long way from here. Perhaps in an adjoining county, if she knows of someone prepared to give her sanctuary.'

'You clearly have important tidings to relate,' said Francis, sitting up, 'and you will do so all the more fluently if your throat is moistened with some of this fine ale. No doubt you are dry of mouth, for to judge by the state of your boots and hose you have ridden hard through a bog, and perhaps a few sandpits for good measure.'

'Ale, certainly,' Edward agreed, and Ralph disappeared into the scullery to fill another pot from the hogshead that was stored there. Edward took a seat and began to explain his dilemma.

'I rode to Newstead, to ask Byron why he'd released the man Struthers without charge. Before I was even able to enquire, I was advised that someone had witnessed you and I removing Rose and all her possessions from Papplewick. Whether or not we were followed to Daybrook I know not, but I strongly suspect that it was Struthers who witnessed our departure, and that he bought his freedom with that information.'

'So that's why you want me to ride to Daybrook?' Francis asked. 'To warn Rose that her hiding place may be known? Certainly that will be no hardship, since given the late hour at which I will be likely to arrive, another overnight sojourn suggests itself. The only unfortunate outcome of that will be the lack of sleep.'

'It's far worse than that,' Edward insisted. 'When I reached Newstead, there was a man there as a guest of Byron's. His name is John Kincaid.'

Francis frowned. 'Isn't he in some way connected with witchcraft?'

'He smokes out witches!' Edward barked. 'He's been brought down here from Scotland, possibly by Byron himself, and he's been travelling the realm exposing witches and having them executed. It seems that he's performed similar services for the Scots King James.'

'But if Rose is not a witch, what has she to lose by being tested?'

'Would *you* trust anyone employed by those who believe in witchcraft and devilry? We have no way of knowing what trickery this mountebank Kincaid employs in order to please his masters, and expose the innocent as something they are not.'

'What was Byron's reaction to learning that you and I had spirited her away?' Francis asked.

'I managed to convince him that I had her safe under the Shire Hall, and that she should only be condemned after a test of her alleged witchery was conducted in full public view, and following any evidence that might exist regarding the evil she is alleged to have wrought on the Newstead estate. I have simple answers to most of those accusations, but there remains the risk that this man Kincaid has trickery of his own designed to make Rose appear to be a witch.'

'Yet you wish me to urge Rose to flee?' Francis said with a frown. 'When is she to be presented for trial — at the next assize?'

'No — seven days from today, which will be next Tuesday.'

'And if she is not?'

'Then I shall be dismissed from office, and perhaps even put on trial myself, should it be suspected that I was the one responsible for her escape.'

'And you are sending *me* to perform that task?' Francis replied accusingly. 'If it ever comes out that I urged her to flee, or was in some way responsible for her evading justice, then *I* shall be the one dismissed from office. You surely push the bounds of friendship, Edward.'

'Do you wish to see a harmless woman hanged?' Edward challenged him. 'Would you sit idly by while the sister of the woman whose bed you occupy is hanged in full public view in order to satisfy the warped mind of Sheriff Byron?'

'Kitty would surely take it ill were I to fail to give Rose such assistance as I can,' Francis admitted, 'so perhaps I should do as you suggest. It's a fine night out there, if a little cool, but the moon is waxing and should afford some light on the track. Where do you wish Rose to take herself off to?'

'I have no suggestion,' Edward sighed, 'since I know little of her background. She may have family in an adjoining county, or a friend somewhere who has access to a boat that could take her down the Trent, into the Humber, and from there safely into the Low Countries, where Popish nonsense regarding witches and ghosts has long since been abandoned. In short, she must decide where she goes. Perhaps she can advise you of where she intends to head, in order that we may locate her later, once common sense has prevailed.'

Francis began preparing to depart, and Edward untied his horse and led it across Whitefriars Lane to his own house, where Elizabeth was waiting for him at the door with a frown.

'Are we so low in your order of priorities that you chose to report your safe return to a friend before reassuring the woman who gave birth to your children that she still has a husband? I suppose you're only here because Meg's suppers are better than Ralph's?'

'Fie, woman, you do me an injustice, and it has been a day that I would rather forget,' Edward replied testily.

Elizabeth stepped back to get a better look at him. She took in the mud-splattered boots and hose and asked, 'How went matters at Newstead?'

'Byron is determined to have an innocent woman hanged as a witch, and I am equally determined that he will not succeed.'

Just then, they heard the sound of a horse being cantered hard up Whitefriars Lane, and Elizabeth peered out into the night. 'Was that Francis?'

'It was, and he is on a mission from me, to warn the lady in question to hide herself away.'

'You've involved Francis in some unwise scheme to preserve a witch?'

'No, I've sent him to save the life of the woman whose simples enabled Robert to talk and eat normally — the sister of Francis's current bedmate, and perhaps his future sister-in-law. Now, do I get any supper, or do I have to take myself to The Bell for fresh bread, ripe cheese and willing prostitutes?'

'The bread and cheese you can get here,' Elizabeth replied, 'but as for the rest, we have none. Come away in, before I change my mind.'

The following morning, Edward was examining the list of overnight arrests in his chamber in the basement of the Shire Hall when he heard urgent footsteps coming down the hallway. He looked up in surprise as Francis appeared breathlessly at the doorway.

'It's barely daylight,' Edward said. 'You must have set off back here at dead of night, assuming that you even made it to Daybrook in the first place. Did you pass on my message to Rose? Has she got somewhere she can escape to? And did Kitty reject your advances?'

'As for Kitty, she was most put out that I had to leave her in order to return here without delay.'

'And why did you need to do that?' Edward asked in alarm. 'Has Rose been taken up by Byron and his servants?'

'Who knows?' Francis replied as he spread his arms wide. 'Rose disappeared two days ago on one of Kitty's ponies, taking only a few possessions and enough food for two days. She's lost to us, Edward, and I had no opportunity to warn her of the new danger she's in!'

10

'Just when I was beginning to think that matters couldn't get any worse,' Edward groaned. 'What are we going to do?'

'Well, since I'm lying with Rose's sister, the least I can do is find her for you.'

'May I take that as an offer on your part to return to Daybrook and begin enquiries, bearing in mind the risk that wherever you go you'll be followed?'

Francis looked puzzled. 'Why would your sheriff order that I be followed, if he believes Rose to be in custody here in Nottingham?'

Edward shook his head sadly. 'I fear that Byron may no longer trust me. I certainly wouldn't, were I in his position. But quite apart from finding Rose, and accounting in some way for her absence from the cells here, how do we prepare to combat Kincaid?'

'Do we need to, if Rose won't be available for testing?'

'Of *course* we need to,' Edward replied. 'For one thing, even if we don't find her, Byron will, in due course, unless she's taken ship to the Low Countries. But we also need to suppress any suggestion that this part of the realm has suddenly fallen under the spell of Satan and his assistants. You may have forgotten that we have yet to come up with a rational explanation for the nightly manifestations at Gallows Hill. I'm beginning to believe that they are in some way connected with Byron's obsession with finding a witch on his own estate.'

Francis looked thoughtful. 'The only person I can think of who might share that view, and who has any authority in Nottingham, is Sheriff Stokely,' he said. 'He'll certainly not be pleased to learn that Byron is determined to smoke out witches along with this new man he's playing host to — Kincaid.'

'Indeed, and there's something about the man that makes the hairs on the back of my neck stand up,' Edward said with a shudder. 'Perhaps we'd better go and see your sheriff.'

Stokely agreed to see them immediately when they told his steward that the matter concerned the upcoming 'trial' of a witch in the Shire Hall. He listened with increasing gloom to what they had to impart regarding Rose's disappearance and Byron's seeming obsession with having her exposed for her alleged evil. When they'd finished, he sighed.

'Regarding the disappearance of this woman Rose, what do you propose to tell Byron?' he asked.

'As little as possible,' Edward replied. 'We just have to hope that he doesn't learn that we don't have her in safe confinement.'

'And if he does?' Stokely challenged him. 'What then? The hue and cry? And if she's caught, will not her flight be taken as evidence of her guilt? Will Byron not claim that she must have disappeared on her besom, or transformed herself into her familiar?' Stokely glanced nervously towards the closed chamber door, then lowered his voice. 'Do you not have someone in custody who looks the part? If the Shire Hall records are as lax as those maintained in the Guildhall — and don't attempt to deny it, Barton — then once you have a woman down there marked off as "Rose", no-one would be likely to ask questions, would they?'

'You're advising that I falsify my gaol records?' Edward asked, slightly shocked.

'It's not for me to advise on how matters are conducted within the county, clearly, but I merely point out that you may shortly be called upon to demonstrate that you have a woman in custody named Rose something or other.'

'Rose Middleham,' Edward informed him. 'I assume that Sheriff Kniveton will not have any interest in the matter?'

'A very bold assumption,' Stokely replied, 'given the man's obsession with the old ways, if I may call them that. Popery, if I am to be less polite. He will almost certainly be in communication with Byron, and the two of them almost certainly serve other masters. It will have been those who arranged for Kincaid to travel the country, discovering witches. Whether they believe in them or not is neither here nor there. Their strings are being pulled by interests much closer to the centre of power in the nation.'

When both men looked blank, Stokely nodded towards the chamber door. 'Barton, would you please ensure that what I am about to tell you will not be overheard? And before I do so, you must both swear an oath to communicate it no further.'

'We swear,' Edward assured him, while Francis checked behind the chamber door and confirmed that there was no-one eavesdropping on the other side. Nevertheless, Stokely lowered his voice to almost a whisper.

'This recent nonsense regarding witches has been whipped up for a purpose that I cannot disclose, but it owes much to the current uncertainty in court circles regarding who will succeed Queen Elizabeth.'

'We've already come across examples of that,' Edward told him, 'under my predecessor. That necessitated us both travelling into Leicestershire, where we were party to unearthing a group of men posing as travelling players, but in truth were intent on putting a pretender on the throne after our current queen's death.'

'Say nothing regarding the possible demise of the queen,' Stokely advised, 'lest it be accounted treason. The matter is obviously a delicate one, and I can only tell you as much as you need to know in order to assist those who wish to see an orderly transition of royal power when … when the time is appropriate.'

'So those who are stirring up a fear of witches — and who may even be accountable for recent events at Gallows Hill — are seeking to promote their own chosen successor to Queen Elizabeth?' Edward asked.

'You have the nub of it,' Stokely confirmed. 'Which is why you must not only unmask this trickery for what it is, but also pass on what you know to those in a position to act upon it.'

'Surely that is something you can undertake, if we keep you regularly informed?' Edward suggested.

Stokely shook his head. 'Would that I could, but any movement on my part to communicate with a man who has been sent from London to investigate, and hopefully put a stop to these matters, would reveal me to our enemies.'

'Who is this man, and who has sent him?' Edward asked eagerly.

'I can tell you only his name, and where he may currently be found. Even I dare not even hint at who has sent him. But perhaps one of you could be my messenger. It will require some colourable excuse for you to travel out of the county, into Leicestershire and to a place called Ashby de la Zouche.'

Edward's eyes widened, and despite himself he let out a hoot of delight that seemed to startle Stokely.

'You know of the place?'

'I have been there!' Edward told him. 'On a family visit, as it transpires. My wife Elizabeth was raised on the estate, where her father was the steward to the Hastings family, while her mother served as housekeeper. They are retired now, and living in a grace-and-favour cottage on the estate, but I was under the impression that the Hastings family had moved on, and that the castle is in ruins.'

'That was the case until recently,' Stokely said, 'and in fact the direct line, and with it the title of Earl of Huntingdon, was passed sideways when the second earl died without issue. They are both now held by George Hastings as the fourth earl, and he has begun restoration work. He is the former High Sheriff of Leicestershire and Knight of the Shire, and although he and his wife and children are most frequently to be found in Gopsall, on the north side of Leicester itself, Sir George is currently in residence at Ashby, supervising much-needed renovation. This has brought many journeymen and skilled builders to the place, and this in turn provides a perfect cover for the man who has been sent from London. His name is Matthew Parkin, and I have been asked to maintain lines of communication with him, since in Ashby he is well placed to keep an eye on the centre of the plot that is unfolding, which is being hatched in Derbyshire. It sounds like you, Mountsorrel, will be the perfect man to send as my messenger, under the guise of making a family visit. I will give you a letter of introduction to Sir George, perhaps hinting that it will be safe to let you meet with Matthew Parkin.'

'Elizabeth *will* be pleased,' Francis said with a smirk.

'She will until she learns that yet again I have used a visit to her parents as an excuse to become involved in courtly intrigue. If you recall, on the previous occasion we were obliged to take refuge in a church in the village of my birth.'

'I recall it well,' said Francis, 'since you were there reunited with your birth mother.'

'For all the time that was granted to us,' Edward murmured sadly, recalling her tragic death. 'But be that as it may, I should clearly lose no time in making plans to depart south of here.'

'Don't forget that you must first find someone to occupy a cell under the Shire Hall,' Stokely reminded them both. 'And that you have only a week to produce the real Rose Middleham.'

'Is this some ruse to get back into my good humour?' Elizabeth demanded suspiciously, when Edward suggested a visit to Ashby. 'Robert was still at my breast the last time I saw my parents, and you always claim to be too occupied with your duties to find the time to embark on a journey that is less than a day's ride. Has this something to do with your office again?'

'Yes and no,' Edward replied evasively. 'Once we are there I shall need to report to the castle, with a letter of introduction to the Earl of Huntingdon from Sheriff Stokely.'

'Not Sheriff Byron?'

'No, Sheriff Stokely, but do not advise anyone else of that.'

'I *knew* it!' Elizabeth said bitterly. 'This has nothing to do with wanting to visit my family.'

'Do you want to go or not?'

'Of course I do, but I do not want to get caught up in any of your intrigues. And don't drag me into any more church lofts, like you did before.'

'This will be perfectly straightforward,' Edward insisted, as he crossed his fingers behind his back. 'It's a simple matter of delivering a message.'

'For a sheriff you don't even work for,' she pointed out. 'And what will Sheriff Byron have to say regarding your absence?'

'Hopefully he'll never know — so just tell Meg that we're visiting your family, which of course we will be.'

'A pity you never get around to calling them *our* family,' Elizabeth grumbled.

Francis led the way down the stairs into the dank corridor below ground level in the Guildhall where they housed the prisoners. Once they reached the access door, and Francis took the key from the turnkey and bid him return to the floor above, he updated Edward. 'A woman named Nellie Winters presides over the lowest stew in town — down in Fisher Gate. She's locked away with three of her girls, who are awaiting their fate from the magistrate. Nellie herself has been sentenced to ninety days by Magistrate Wellworthy, and she's only a few days into her sentence. We'll bring her out into the corridor here and put our proposal to her. She's not stupid, and I'm sure she'll be only too delighted to exchange ninety days for a mere seven.'

An hour later, Edward and Francis had finished persuading Nellie to pose as Rose Middleham. The turnkey in charge of the main holding cells under the Shire Hall recoiled in disgust from the smell of the old crone whose oaths and curses could be heard as she was pushed down the stairs by Edward, with Francis prodding her onwards with the end of his staff of office.

Edward handed Nellie over to the turnkey. 'Don't get downwind of her,' he warned the man, 'or else you'll find that you've lost your appetite for dinner. I've smelt pigsties with more allure.'

The turnkey held his breath and steered Nellie towards the open cell door. He slammed the door behind her, then turned back to Edward and Francis.

'You were right about the smell from the old sow, but I've smelt worse. And it won't put me off my dinner.'

'Talking of dinner,' Francis said, as he and Edward returned to ground level, 'it's your turn to buy the meat pies, to celebrate a successful ruse.'

The delight on the faces of Edwin and Catherine Porter showed as clearly as their surprise to see the horse and wagon rumble up to the door of their home in the former gatehouse to Ashby Castle. Elizabeth gave an excited shout, jumped down and embraced her mother, while her father reached up and lifted Robert down before assisting Margaret to jump onto the dusty ground.

'My, you've grown apace, young feller!' Edwin proclaimed as he looked Robert up and down proudly. 'You'll soon be as tall as your father.'

'But not as neglectful of his family, if I get my way,' Elizabeth asserted as she hugged her father and shouted to Edward to lift down their travelling bags.

'You're too hard on the poor man,' Catherine scolded her. 'Hasn't he just brought you here, and hasn't he provided you with a good home in which to raise your children?'

'A home that only occasionally contains him,' Elizabeth retorted. 'But enough about that. Are we too late for dinner?'

'You're *never* too late for that,' her mother assured her. 'How long are you staying this time?'

'Ask him.' Elizabeth jerked her head towards Edward, who was lifting down the last of the bags, which Edwin was transferring into the humble two-roomed cottage.

An hour later, Edwin and Edward sat outside watching Margaret chasing Robert up and down the grass strip that led to the small vegetable garden to the rear.

'Would you care for some beer?' Edwin asked. 'Then perhaps you could tell me why my daughter has taken so badly to the hours you must have to spend away from home in the furtherance of your duties. She's obviously forgotten that she hardly saw her father from one end of the day to the other in her youth.'

'Perhaps that is why she is upset with me,' Edward suggested as he accepted the foaming mug and downed the contents in one swallow. 'But those days have recently been revived at Ashby Castle, or so I hear,' he observed.

Edwin nodded. 'The latest Earl of Huntingdon is highly favoured by the queen, and enjoys considerable wealth from his many offices. In my day, the castle was forever receiving visitors from court, and it was only when the second earl's health failed him, and the title passed to his brother, that this ceased, and they had no further use for either myself or Catherine. But now it seems that the fourth earl wishes to restore the past glory of the castle, and I hear that he's appointed a new steward and housekeeper.'

'Does the earl have many visitors?' Edward asked.

Edwin shrugged. 'Lots of folk travelling up and down the drive, certainly, but I think most of them are stonemasons and suchlike, to judge by their dress. Very few from court, so far as I can tell, but of course I'm not always sitting out here in front of the cottage.'

'And you shouldn't be now, Father,' Elizabeth told him as she emerged from the house to call the children in. 'Dinner's ready.'

Edward waited for three days before he ventured to embark on the commission that had brought him to Ashby, in the hope that he would restore his image as a family man, if it had ever existed. Elizabeth took to eyeing him curiously, as if waiting for him to reveal the real reason for their visit.

But eventually he could delay no longer, and announced after breakfast on the fourth day that he would need to walk up the drive to the castle to deliver a message from Sheriff Stokely to the earl. 'I should be back in time for dinner,' he announced cheerily as he tried to avoid Elizabeth's eyes.

'Let's hope so,' Catherine replied, 'since I'll be cooking up the rest of that lamb, and we have fresh cabbage from the garden.'

An hour later Edward presented himself to the steward of Ashby Castle, advising him that he brought greetings from the Sheriff of Nottingham for his master. He was immediately admitted into the great hall, and was just gazing upwards in fascination at the network of wooden scaffolding on which men were going about various tasks with poles, trowels, compasses and buckets of lime mortar, when a door at the far end opened and in walked a tall, portly man in his late fifties, accompanied by what appeared to be two men at arms. At least, Edward had never before seen footmen carrying swords.

'You bring greetings from Nottingham, I'm advised,' the man said.

Edward gave a half bow. 'If you be the Earl of Huntingdon, then indeed I do. Here is a letter of introduction.'

He handed the scroll over, and Huntingdon read it briefly, then handed it back. 'You are Sheriff Stokely's bailiff?'

'No, my lord — I serve the Sheriff of the County, Sir John Byron.'

He had clearly said the wrong thing, to judge by the sour look on the earl's face, and he hastened to correct any false impression he might have given.

'But my real purpose is to enquire whether or not a certain gentleman named Matthew Parkin might be found here.'

'I thought as much,' the earl declared as he turned to his two attendants. 'Seize this man and take him below.'

11

Edward blinked as his eyes adjusted to the dark, damp cell into which he'd been pushed, prior to the door being slammed behind him. He was wondering how Elizabeth would react to his failure to return at dinnertime, and also how long he would be kept a prisoner. But above all he was wondering what the hell he'd done or said that had landed him down there.

For a brief moment he pondered the possibility that the letter of introduction from Stokely had instructed whoever read it to lock him away. Then common sense prevailed and he reminded himself that the sheriff had sent him on a mission after disclosing certain sensitive information, and would therefore have hardly given instruction that he be incarcerated. Unless, of course, Stokely was working in league with Sheriff Byron, in which case Edward's goose was well and truly cooked. But that didn't make sense either, since Byron was friendly with the other town sheriff, Kniveton, and Stokely could hardly be described as a friend of *his*.

His thoughts were interrupted by a grating noise as the bolt on the door was slid open and a man appeared. He was carrying a burning torch, which he placed in the metal bracket on the stone wall. He then stood looking down at Edward, who was seated with his knees drawn up and his back to the wall.

'Who exactly *are* you?' the man demanded.

'The letter of introduction I gave to that mannerless oaf occupying this building clearly stated who I am,' Edward replied curtly. 'I am bailiff to the Sheriff of Nottinghamshire.'

'But *not* the Sheriff of Nottingham, who supplied you with the letter,' the man pointed out. 'For all we know, that letter was a poor forgery. And why are you seeking a man called Matthew Parkin?'

'That's my business,' Edward replied. 'And since my enquiry regarding whether or not he might be found here was in itself sufficient to have me thrown into this cell, you will forgive me if I decline to elaborate further.'

The man squatted down on his haunches, bringing his face level with Edward's. 'I am Matthew Parkin. How did you know I was here?'

'I was advised of that by Sheriff Stokely, obviously. He wished me to pass on certain information regarding a recent outbreak of supposed witchcraft in Nottingham and the surrounding countryside.'

'Why do you say "supposed"?' Parkin asked.

'Because I am not as gullible as some. Nor do I believe all that Popish piffle about hauntings, and souls returning from the dead.'

'But you have information that might be of value to us?'

'That rather depends on who you mean by *us*,' Edward replied. 'If it includes that miserable bastard who had me thrown in here, then forgive me if I decline to part with anything other than a fart of displeasure.'

'I understand your reluctance,' Parkin replied, as he lowered himself into a seated position on the cold floor, 'and you must make allowances for the earl, who is not the brightest candle in the cathedral on occasions, of which this was one. But you must also cast some of the blame for the misunderstanding on Sheriff Stokely, who said only, in the letter that he gave you, that you were aware of certain facts pertaining to a challenge to the throne. This could clearly be interpreted in more than one way, and the earl should have asked further questions — such as those that I just posed to you — before forming entirely the wrong conclusion. It would seem that the information you can supply does indeed have implications for the succession, but of a nature that accords with our hopes and exertions.'

'I have not the slightest understanding of what you're talking about,' Edward told him testily, 'but I am bound to express my extreme displeasure at the treatment I have thus far been afforded.'

Parkin got back to his feet, took the torch from the wall bracket and hammered on the door for the gaoler to open it up. He turned to Edward before leaving. 'You won't be here a moment longer than necessary.'

An hour later Edward was seated at a heavy dining table in a side chamber from the main hall of Ashby Castle. Before him was a sumptuous spread of assorted meats, fresh bread, fish platters and dishes of fruits, all accompanied by flagons of wine. Seated across from him were the man claiming to be Matthew Parkin, and the Earl of Huntingdon, who was craving Edward's forgiveness for the fifth time.

'We cannot afford to take unnecessary chances, you see. When you learn more of what we can reveal, you will realise why we needed to be so circumspect.'

Edward selected items for his trencher while deciding whether or not to reveal what he knew already, and risk being sent back down to the dark cell. Then it occurred to him that lives other than his own might be implicated, and that the more he could gain the confidence of his host and fellow guest, the better equipped he would be to deal with those matters over which he had some control.

'I have come to suspect that certain recent events in Nottingham might concern the matter of the succession to the throne of England,' he ventured. 'That is, of course, when Her Majesty no longer has need of it. And on a previous occasion I was fortunate enough to be of some assistance to Master Robert Cecil in a similar cause.'

It fell silent until Parkin asked quietly, 'You have met the new Secretary of State?'

'I have indeed,' Edward confirmed. 'On the first occasion he was taking a gift across the border to the King of Scotland, and on the second his father was seeking to suppress what might be described as a bid for the throne, before it fell vacant, by a group who had a claimant of their own.'

Huntingdon and Parkin exchanged uneasy glances, and it was again Parkin who made the necessary enquiry.

'Do you perchance recall who that claimant was?'

'The details are somewhat hazy now, since this was two years or so ago,' Edward replied. 'But from memory it was a young woman who at that time was living on an estate in Derbyshire.'

'She still is,' Parkin replied. 'Her name is Arbella Stuart, and she lives with her grandmother at Hardwick Hall. She is unashamedly of the old religion, and is regarded by many as the best hope for the restoration of Rome on the expiry of the current regime.'

'I am also led to believe that those who oppose Rome look across the Scottish border for the successor when Elizabeth is promoted to glory,' Edward added guardedly.

Parkin nodded. 'Fear not to mention the death of Queen Elizabeth directly, since it will of course occur one day, and we are all loyal subjects.'

'They say she grows less robust with the years,' Edward ventured, and again it was Parkin who dispensed with the diplomacy.

'She grows more feeble, certainly, but she refuses to name a successor, and of course she has no heir. This is why the diplomacy currently being conducted by Cecil is so crucial to a smooth transition when the time comes. A transition to one raised as a Protestant, of course.'

'Even though his mother was a Catholic, and a traitor to England's cause?' Edward queried, and for the first time his remarks seemed to unsettle both men across the board from him.

'Those matters must be conveniently forgotten, should King James agree to accept the Crown of England,' Huntingdon muttered.

Edward inclined his head in acknowledgement. 'So the matter is not settled?' he asked.

'Indeed it is not,' replied Parkin. 'And there are fears that James will be reluctant to accept, which is why recent events in the nation are of such critical importance.'

'I must own that I have some difficulty in understanding the connection between affairs in Scotland and accusations of witchcraft and other devilry in the east Midlands,' Edward admitted.

Parkin helped himself to a generous draught of wine, cleared his throat and embarked on an explanation. 'It began, so far as we have been able to determine, when King James visited Denmark, in order to lay siege to the affections of Princess Anne, who is now his queen following a marriage by proxy at Elsinore, while James was back in Scotland. While in Denmark he became aware of a rapidly developing mania regarding witches, who are regarded as the Devil's agents here on earth. It would seem that the impressionable James became caught up in this, and saw ill portents in every worldly event, most notably the passage of ships across the ocean. When the vessel carrying his bride was forced by storms to seek safe harbour in Norway, James took ship himself to bring her safely back across the North Ocean to Scotland.'

'Very gallant,' Edward murmured. 'But what has this to do with witchcraft?'

'What happened next was regarded by James as a curse upon the Danish royal family and his chosen bride, because of their persecution of witches during his sojourn there. Anyway, as it transpired, his own vessel was caught in a great storm that almost wrecked it, and he became convinced that the Devil had employed witches to stir up the sea between Oslo and Leith, which is the port that serves Edinburgh.'

'So he began searching for them?' Edward asked.

Parkin shook his head. 'He did not need to. Later that same year, a group of Scottish nobles who were seeking to gain favour with James learned of accusations being levelled against a group of women in a village overlooking the southern approaches to Leith — a place called North Berwick. James was easily convinced that they had been responsible for hazarding the lives of himself and his queen, and took a very personal interest in the trials that followed, in which over fifty innocent souls, most of them harmless old women, were brutally tortured, then burned at the stake, for alleged witchcraft.'

'I have learned that the practice in this country is for them to be hanged instead,' Edward observed, to which Parkin responded with a derisive snort.

'They are still put to death, whatever be the chosen manner of it. There is a man currently travelling the nation searching out witches, possibly on the orders of James himself, but equally possibly at the behest of those who wish to make England less attractive to James.'

'John Kincaid?' Edward asked.

The other two men looked shocked.

'You have heard of him?' Parkin asked.

Edward nodded. 'I have actually met him, at the home of my employer, Sheriff Byron.'

'It is worse than we thought,' Parkin muttered to the earl. 'He is even closer to Hardwick, and is no doubt in contact with the Stuart woman. Tell me, Master Mountsorrel, what thought you of Kincaid?'

'A most unpleasant individual,' Edward replied with a shudder. 'He claims to be able to expose witches by pricking their skin, and he has already met with success in various parts of the realm.'

'The device he uses is false,' Parkin spat. 'It has a broad barrel, from which the pricking spike protrudes, and there is said to be a button on the side that allows the blade to retract when it comes into contact with the skin of a suspected witch. Kincaid claims that if an alleged witch is pricked with this device, and does not bleed, then she is indeed a witch, since she is being protected by her lord, Satan himself.'

'So this man Kincaid can turn any chosen victim into a witch, simply by interfering with this pricking spike?'

'Precisely. And of course it is in his interest to expose as many witches as possible, since he is being paid handsomely to do so.'

'By whom?'

'Is it not obvious?' Parkin asked. 'By those who wish to place Arbella Stuart on the throne rather than James of Scotland.'

When Edward looked blankly at the two men across from him, Parkin explained further.

'James will not venture onto the English throne if he believes the nation to be swarming with witches; therefore, it is in the best interests of any rival claimant to portray that as being the case. James's obsession with witches is closely allied with his belief that kingship is a direct gift from God, and that he is appointed by Him to stamp out witchcraft in his own realm. But he is already weary of the task, and rumour has it that he is also afraid that he will bring about his own premature death by meddling with Satan's plans.'

'So his religious beliefs are not as strong as he would have others believe?'

'Seemingly not, because of course his mother was of the old religion, and there is a school of philosophy that asserts that Satan can only be defeated by Rome, and the old Popish procedures for the banishment of evil spirits. The recent emergence and continued prevalence of witches is said to be a direct result of Elizabeth and her predecessors turning their backs on Rome and the old power of the Catholic Church. Those of us who subscribe to the Reformist beliefs know otherwise, of course, but an ignorant population will believe anything if they are whipped into a frenzy of fear regarding dark forces, the Devil's handmaidens, the return of the living dead, and all that superstitious rubbish. So the presence of witches and evil spirits walking the land serves two purposes for the supporters of Arbella Stuart. It discourages James from accepting the English crown, as he is being urged to do by Cecil, and at the same time it encourages people to return to Rome, and the old beliefs.'

'Has Queen Elizabeth been acquainted with these developments?' Edward asked.

Parkin nodded ruefully. 'Indeed she has, but her response has been lukewarm thus far. For one thing, she will not formally acknowledge that James is her rightful successor, and that there is accordingly a need to suppress those forces that might cause him to decline. And for another, she is fearful of being considered intolerant of those whose religious views are not her own. Put another way, she hesitates to declaim processes that have existed within the Roman Church for centuries designed to combat the forces of evil — what some call exorcism. There is even a risk that her enemies might claim that she has herself been responsible for the recent alleged increase in witchcraft and other devilry because of the laxity of her efforts to combat it.'

'But she passed a law against it, did she not?'

'Indeed she did,' Parkin conceded, 'but it lacks teeth. Firstly, it does not prescribe burning as the mode of death if convicted. Secondly — and this has proved a considerable handicap in stamping out witchcraft — even hanging is not to be inflicted unless it can be proved that the witchcraft in question led to the death of a victim. You can readily understand how such a mild response to a perceived evil that threatens the realm could lead to accusations that Her Majesty is herself a witch. It is doubly unfortunate that she is known to keep secret company with a Doctor John Dee, an alchemist and mathematician who openly boasts that he can raise the Devil from slumber.'

'While she prevaricates in this manner,' the earl added, 'there are clear exhortations in the Scriptures that those who have what is called a "familiar spirit" should "surely be put to death". You can understand the concern of those of us who have the welfare of England at heart.'

'Indeed,' Edward muttered, 'and I can now understand why Sheriff Stokely wished for matters in Nottinghamshire to be brought to your urgent attention.'

'What precisely has been happening?' Parkin asked.

Edward told him of the wild scenes at the hanging, and the subsequent ghostly manifestations that had resulted in the nightly attendances of credulous crowds at Gallows Hill. 'A wise woman from the north of the town has also been accused by Sheriff Byron of being a witch, and he set me the task of taking her into custody ahead of her being put to the test by Kincaid.'

'And you have done so?' Parkin asked.

Edward shook his head. 'I have created the impression that she is safely in custody, but if the truth be known she has been allowed to escape, and my colleague Bailiff Barton, from the town, is currently attempting to find her.'

'You mean that he is pretending to search for her?' Parkin persisted. 'She is in fact securely hidden away by you?'

'No,' Edward admitted. 'I am ashamed to admit that she fled of her own accord when we declined to take her into custody. But Sheriff Byron believes that we have her secure, and has ordered her public examination by Kincaid next Tuesday.'

Parkin's eyebrows rose in alarm. 'She must not be examined by Kincaid at any cost, even if you have to forfeit your office. Do we have your undertaking on that?'

'Of course,' Edward assured him. 'Quite apart from any other consideration, I do not consider her to be a witch. A wise woman certainly, but no witch.'

'And what about these nightly manifestations of which you spoke?' the earl asked. 'Have you taken steps to investigate them, hopefully with a view to proving that they are mere dramatic illusions created by those in the pay of those seeking to deter King James from accepting the throne?'

'I have witnessed them for myself,' Edward replied, 'and I am obliged to admit that they are skilfully executed. However, I have yet to determine how they are produced.'

'This must be your first priority,' said Parkin. 'If we can demonstrate that what the gullible regard as true manifestations of the Devil are in fact sleight of hand — the stock-in-trade of theatrical players — then we shall be well on the way to exposing Kincaid as a common mountebank, and sending him back to King James with his tail between his legs. We might even go further, and have him tried here in England for false practices.'

'I shall do as you request,' Edward agreed, 'although I cannot guarantee success.'

'You are well aware of what is at stake,' said Parkin gravely, 'and should you be removed from office by Sheriff Byron you will receive support from London, on that you may rely. And now perhaps we should not delay you any further, if you have dined sufficiently.'

'Indeed I have, and my most gracious thanks for a splendid dinner,' Edward said as he rose from the table. 'I must now face the wrath of my wife and her family for forswearing a more humble repast.'

Back at the Porters' cottage, as the sun began its slow descent to the west, the reception from Elizabeth was all that he had glumly anticipated on his walk back from the castle.

'Little wonder that my mother now begins to believe my tales of neglect and abandonment,' she hissed as she emerged from the cottage. 'At the very least you must apologise most abjectly for being absent from a most delicious dinner. And don't for one moment imagine that we saved you some.'

'As a matter of fact, I dined with the Earl of Huntingdon,' Edward said with a smirk, then wished he hadn't as Elizabeth knocked his bonnet from his head.

'You are a lout and a totally unsuitable husband,' she declared.

Edward was in the process of rescuing his bonnet from the grass when she added, 'And I think I'd prefer to stay here with the children, rather than journey back with you to a house that is always missing your presence. Go back alone and attend to those duties that you clearly regard as more important than being a husband and father. Perhaps your sheriff will think more highly of you if you devote *every* hour of each day to your alleged duties, rather than most of them. You may even receive preferment from London.'

'Indeed I might,' Edward muttered as he entered the cottage. 'But not for the reasons that you imagine.'

12

Edward's first call upon his return to Whitefriars Lane was to Francis's house, hopeful that he might have good news regarding his search for Rose Middleham. The door was opened by Francis's houseboy Ralph, who frowned when he saw Edward.

'Is your master at home?' Edward asked.

Ralph shook his head. 'I haven't seen him since you was last here, and he rode off north somewhere. I was hoping that you were him, 'cos it's not like him to be missing for so long and I'm starting to get worried that something's happened to him.'

Somewhat alarmed, Edward thanked Ralph, told him not to worry, then walked his horse thoughtfully across to his own house. Meg emerged through the scullery door from her accommodation next to the garden kitchen when she heard the sound of Edward moving through the rooms lighting rush lamps.

'Are the mistress and children not with you?' she asked.

Edward explained that they'd remained in Ashby because he had important duties to attend to that would keep him from the house for long hours. 'If I'm home in the mornings, just put out some breakfast for me, but don't worry about dinner and supper,' he told her. 'I'll arrange to eat out somewhere.'

'Good news for the pie sellers,' Meg muttered as she went back to her bed, leaving Edward to help himself from the hogshead of small beer in the scullery and take a seat before the empty fireplace while he gathered his thoughts.

The fact that Francis had been absent for so long suggested that he was experiencing difficulty in locating Rose; either that or he'd found her, and she was refusing to come back into town to face accusations of witchcraft. He could not blame her if that was the case. But it was now only two days before the date set for Rose's 'trial'. If it was discovered that she had fled, this in itself would suggest a guilty knowledge on her part, and would further deepen the general belief that witchcraft was prevalent in the county.

This would serve the interests of those seeking to deter King James of Scotland from accepting the English crown, even assuming that he was to be offered it. It would suit the supporters of the woman called Arbella Stuart equally well for Rose to remain hidden, so that she could be accused of witchcraft in her absence. And even if by some miracle she could be located and brought into Nottingham, there was an equal risk that John Kincaid would employ trickery, lies and false witnesses to justify having Rose condemned and hanged as a servant of Satan.

It was a hopeless outlook whichever way it went, and there was now a distinct possibility that Francis, by absenting himself around the county and searching openly for Rose, would reveal to anyone dogging his movements that the lady in question was missing. When — and if — Sheriff Byron learned that, Edward would no longer be employed as his bailiff, and would be unable to do anything more to ensure Rose's safety. And how long before Francis's prolonged absence from his duties in the town provoked a similar response from Sheriff Kniveton? If he sought to dismiss Francis, would Sheriff Stokely have the courage to block such an action, and did he have the authority to do so in the first place?

Edward fell asleep in the chair before the cold fireplace, and awoke, stiff and chilled, to the sound of Meg clattering dishes in the scullery. He rose and stretched, and Meg poked her head around the door and asked if Edward was needing breakfast. Several slices of slightly stale bread and equally tired cheese later, Edward thanked her and walked outside into a pale autumn sunlight to retrieve his horse from the stable down the side of the house. He looked down at the modest orchard, visualised Margaret and Robert chasing each other through the trees, and with considerable effort suppressed his mounting feelings of loneliness and despair.

His first destination was the Guildhall, where the constables on day duty confirmed that Francis had not been seen for days, but assured him that they were organising the duties between themselves. Edward commended them on their devotion, and instructed that should any matter arise that would normally require Francis's attention, he could be found in his chamber below the Shire Hall, to which he took himself without further delay.

Edward was sifting through the reports that had collected in his absence from constables in outlying villages — who in the main had nothing more serious to report than small stock thefts, alehouse brawls and stealing from barns and orchards — when a red-faced Sheriff Kniveton appeared in the open doorway.

'I was told I could find you here, which is of course where you should be. Which is more than can be said for that lazy scoundrel Barton. Where exactly *is* he? And don't try to pretend that you don't know, because you two are as thick as curds in a milk jug.'

'I have not the slightest idea where he may be,' Edward answered honestly. 'But if it will set your mind at rest, I've left word with the constables in the Guildhall that any matter requiring a bailiff's attention may be referred to me in the meantime. I understand that Francis has been absent for several days, so if you wish, I'll conduct my own enquiries into his whereabouts. For all we know, he's been set upon, and his body hidden away, or perhaps cast into the Trent.'

'If you think that smooth collection of expertly woven lies has succeeded in averting my suspicions, then think again!' Kniveton blustered. 'The slovenly man has clearly gone off on some enterprise of his own, probably one involving another plump widow. He's been warned against this more than once, and as a God-fearing servant of the true Redeemer I've prayed for his deliverance from the sins of carnal temptation. But my Christian charity can only be extended so far, and when it threatens to prejudice the rightful performance of the duties of my honourable office I must of course resist the temptation to play the Good Samaritan. You may choose to visit wherever he is currently shirking his responsibilities, and advise him that if he is not at his post by this time on the morrow, he will forfeit his office. Good day to you.'

'Farty-bladder,' Edward muttered under his breath as Kniveton's footsteps receded. Up on the ground level, the sheriff could be heard advising the duty constable in a loud voice that should any word come regarding the whereabouts of Town Bailiff Barton, it was to be relayed to him without delay. Edward sighed and turned his attention back to the reports on his desk, only to be interrupted once again by the Shire Hall doorkeeper.

'Sorry to disturb you, sir, but the town sheriff would like to have a word with you.'

'He already did,' Edward replied testily. 'Several words, actually — all of them impolite and none of them encouraging.'

'Not Sheriff Kniveton, sir — the other one, Stokely.'

'By all means show him in. And please bring down a chair more suitable for a shrieval backside than that bench in front of my desk that normally only serves for miscreants.'

The doorkeeper followed Edward's orders, and Stokely was soon ushered into the room.

'Should anyone enquire,' Stokely said quietly as he made himself comfortable, 'I am merely seeking information regarding the likely whereabouts of Bailiff Barton. Though of course I wish to learn what you can tell me of your recent visit to Ashby.'

'As regards Barton,' Edward said with a grimace, 'I can tell you only that in accordance with your suggestion we installed a woman in the cells here posing as Rose Middleham, and Francis set off in search of the real one. I have heard nothing, either *of* or *from* him, since then, and am growing a little apprehensive that he may have met with foul play. From what I learned in Ashby, we are dealing with more than a vindictive county sheriff in this matter.'

'Indeed. Were you advised of the possible connection with a certain estate in Derbyshire?'

'I was, and it served to clarify certain thoughts in my mind. The allegations against Rose Middleham may perhaps have their origins in the vengeful spite of a woman named Agnes Merryweather, whose path Rose crossed on an occasion in the past. However, the recent events on Gallows Hill are more probably intended to unsettle the community, and lead to fears that Nottinghamshire has joined other areas of the nation in playing host to dark forces, thereby reducing by one the number of possible candidates for the inheritance of the English crown.'

'It is as well that you speak circumspectly of such matters,' Stokely said, 'but what strategy do you intend to adopt in order to uncover the truth regarding the goings-on at Gallows Hill? Once the next assizes are over there will no doubt be other hangings, and further opportunities for theatrical diversions.'

'That point had occurred to me,' Edward admitted, 'and I intend to recommence my enquiries in that direction, beginning this very night.'

'Not alone, I hope?'

'Indeed not. I intend to take two of your town constables with me. I would have preferred Francis Barton by my side, obviously, but I doubt that he will return by sunset today. You should know that if he is not here by cock-crow tomorrow, Sheriff Kniveton has it in mind to dismiss him from office. Can he do so without your consent?'

Stokely shrugged. 'The appointment of a bailiff is a joint matter, on which we must both be in agreement, so I imagine that a dismissal requires the same formality. Francis Barton was in post when Kniveton and I took up our appointments, so in the same way that Sheriff Byron inherited you, we inherited him. But I would need a good reason for retaining his services — a good *official* reason, that is.'

'We may be able to blame his current absence on the escape from custody of Rose Middleham, and the need for him to go in search of her. This will of course place me in bad odour with Sheriff Byron, but I no doubt will be anyway, once all this is over.'

'Once all this is over, I doubt Sir John Byron will even *be* the county sheriff,' said Stokely. 'For that matter, I doubt he will retain his knightly status, or indeed his head. Championing a Catholic contender for the throne of England during the continuing reign of a Protestant incumbent might be accounted treason.'

The full moon threw eerie shadows across the gallows as Edward and his two accompanying constables squatted in the same line of bushes that Edward had employed on the previous occasion, and which sat alongside the hangman's cottage.

Edward shifted his position slightly and whispered to his two companions. 'When the performance begins, try to ignore it and watch for any suspicious movement, particularly to the side of that copse of trees in which I expect the manifestations to be centred. And remember that it's all make-believe — none of it can harm you.'

Before long the crowd of people who were amassed on the uneven ground ahead of their hiding place began to grow restless. Some members of the audience began calling out mockingly, with cries of 'Where are you tonight, dead folk?' and 'Satan cut your tongues out, has he?'

As if in response, several bright red flames shot up through the trees, accompanied by a hideous grinding noise, as if the gates of Hell were being slowly opened. Then a red-eyed skull appeared in mid-air in the middle of the copse, and a mocking voice bellowed out at them.

'Mock while you are able, puny ones! Your souls are forfeit to the Prince of Darkness, and we who were cruelly and unjustly done to death on this cursed spot will drag you down into the eternal flames, there to endure the tortures of the damned. You pour scorn upon us now, but you will shortly join us for all time coming, pleading for a mercy that will never be granted you. My sisters here on earth will put the cursed mark on you, each in turn, *then* shall you learn of the lies preached by false prophets who have led this nation into Purgatory with their blasphemies. Prepare yourselves, sisters, and go out among them. Bring back souls for the flames!'

This was followed by a loud cackling, which was all that it took for the nervous crowd that had previously been baying for entertainment to scatter in all directions, crying out for mercy. 'Keep your eyes peeled!' Edward exhorted his companions as they watched the chaos from the safety of their hiding place, but he had overestimated their courage, and looked on in helpless rage as they too fled.

Cursing wildly, he forced himself to concentrate on what was happening in front of him, and was rewarded when he caught sight of a furtive shadow travelling against the flow. Whereas everyone else seemed to be fighting to exit Gallows Hill by way of the two roads that met there, one figure was slinking from the copse of trees that had played host to the recent display and towards Thomas Gullen's cottage.

Edward rose quickly and broke through the foliage, racing to head off whoever it might be, entertaining his own strong suspicions. He was proved correct when he found himself face to face with a red-faced Gullen, and he drew his sword as he commanded him to remain where he was.

'Not fearful for your own soul, then?' he asked the hangman, and for a moment Gullen seemed to be lost for words. Then he appeared to pull himself together.

'Aren't you? If you witnessed what I just did, then we're *both* doomed, and it's your fault for ordering me to keep watch.'

'You could have done that from the safety of your cottage,' Edward reminded him, 'so why did you venture into the very place from which the demons were emerging?'

'I were only doing my duty,' Gullen complained, 'and now my soul's forfeit, and you'll be needing a new hangman.'

'I'll probably be needing one for a very different reason,' Edward replied. 'I'll be back with reinforcements, on that you may depend. And *then* we'll get to the bottom of all this.'

13

Edward spent a restless night pondering what best to do in the circumstances. His concern for Rose Middleham had led him into a mess that seemed impossible to untangle. Not only that, but he'd almost certainly been responsible for Francis being dismissed from office unless he could come up with some valid excuse for his lengthy absence from duty.

In two days' time Edward would be called upon to produce Rose for public examination by the almost certainly corrupt John Kincaid, who was not only driven by ambition and greed to expose innocent women to accusations of witchcraft, but was also being encouraged by Sheriff Byron to have Rose condemned and executed. It had become obvious to Edward that Byron was not simply a superstitious and gullible believer in the presence of dark forces around his estate, but was in some way in league with those further north in Derbyshire who were plotting to present Arbella Stuart as a suitable candidate for the throne of England, and the person who would bring back the 'old faith' for those zealous Catholics who'd been tolerated, but no more, by Queen Elizabeth.

When the truth emerged that Rose was not, as Edward had pretended, safely locked away beneath the Shire Hall, then he too would also be dismissed from office, and perhaps even charged with some offence by a vengeful and unforgiving Byron. Edward knew no other trade, having been a soldier in the service of Robert Dudley, Earl of Leicester, before becoming a bailiff. Dudley had died within weeks of the defeat of the Spanish Armada, and could no longer be called upon to give a letter of reference for Edward, whose only other employment prior to his enlistment had been on the land, which he was now too old to resume, even if someone were prepared to give employment to a disgraced former bailiff. Elizabeth would almost certainly opt to remain in Ashby with the children, and he shuddered as he imagined facing her with news of his fall from financial security.

He rose early, instructed Meg to go back to her bed when she appeared in the scullery, and after swallowing some bread smeared with dripping from some pork that she had cooked the previous day he set off dolefully for his chamber under the Shire Hall, determined to leave a clean desk ahead of his almost certain forced departure. He had decided to tell the truth, in the hope that he might at least preserve Francis, and his pride insisted that when he was obliged to vacate his own office there should be nothing left unattended to.

He cast his eyes over the latest reports, subconsciously noting their contents and signing off on them when they seemed not to call for any further action on his part. Those accused of routine transgressions such as alehouse brawling, minor thieving and vagrancy could be held in the various village lock-ups in which they were currently languishing until the nearest magistrate ordered them to be fined, whipped, pilloried or driven from the parish, while the only two serious matters — an assault in Southwell and a robbery in Kirkby — had already been slated for the county assize that was scheduled for the Michaelmas term.

He almost missed it as his eyes flitted across the report from outlying Newark. It was the word 'player'. A group of travelling entertainers had been apprehended by Edward's two Newark constables on charges of vagrancy. It was a matter for each individual parish how to deal with those who occasionally appeared among them with their painted wagons and flat boards laid on a village green as a temporary stage, offering such diversions as juggling, acrobatics, musical performances and dramas in which the 'players' recreated heroic characters from history. Having posed as a travelling player himself several years previously, in order to infiltrate a group of traitors, Edward had some limited sympathy for them, and had instructed the constables in his county to tolerate such displays provided that there was no outbreak of the evils normally attendant upon such arrivals, such as prostitution, intemperance, sneak thieving, dice-cogging and sales of pondwater masquerading as cure-alls.

This group in Newark, calling themselves the 'Lincoln Players', had abused this conditional tolerance when two of the ladies travelling as part of the company had brazenly offered additional 'entertainment' to local men in the back yard of the Black Swan after dark, and for sixpence a head. These women, along with the leader of the group, one Henry Burridge, had been arrested and thrown into the lock-up under the Newark Trade Hall, and local constable Nicholas Thrumpton was seeking Edward's consent to have them dealt with in the local Petty Sessions Court. Instead, Edward drafted a despatch requesting that Burridge be transferred to the Shire Hall on a charge of brothel-keeping, which was a Quarter Sessions matter. Not that Edward intended to list the matter; instead he hoped to bargain with Burridge, exchanging a reduction in charges for some expert information on how to stage dramatic effects. He also gave instructions for Nellie Winters to be released, with thanks from him and a few shillings for her trouble.

Edward was enjoying his renewed optimism when his ebullience was shattered by a commanding voice in his open doorway.

'I thought it best to confront you here, rather than call for you to visit me, and perhaps get lost on the way to Newstead!' Sheriff Byron announced as he strode through the door, followed by John Kincaid and Sheriff Kniveton. 'Where is the witch who calls herself Magic Mary, or has she disappeared into thin air as well?'

'As well as whom?' Edward asked innocently. The moment had come, but a few hours earlier than he'd anticipated.

'You know full well who!' Kniveton yelled from behind Byron's shoulder. 'That do-nothing who calls himself my bailiff, but who shall be seeking other means of livelihood before this day is ended. Barton — where is he?'

'I have no knowledge of his precise whereabouts,' Edward admitted, 'but I can tell you what business he's engaged upon.'

'Witch business?' Kincaid asked.

'Witch business indeed,' Edward confirmed. 'He's searching for the woman called Magic Mary.'

'The witch who you assured me you had secured in the cells here?' Byron demanded.

'The very same. She *was* here when I gave you that assurance, but two nights ago she somehow escaped. I am at a loss to understand how, since I had a man guarding her cell door, and another at the door that leads to the cells.'

'It is no mystery, perhaps,' Kincaid suggested, 'since women of her sort can turn themselves into their familiars with a flick of their fingers. She no doubt passed herself off as a rat, of which I have no doubt you have a plentiful supply down here.'

'It may be as you suggest,' Edward replied with a nod, silently thanking the garrulous Kincaid for supplying the answer to the next difficult question he'd been anticipating.

'So why did you send Barton in search of her, rather than undertaking that task yourself?' Kniveton demanded. 'This left the town without an effective guardian of the public peace.'

'And it does not reflect well on my office when my bailiff is obliged to rely on another to perform his duties,' Byron added. 'So I *also* enquire — why send him?'

'Because he is not as well known in the outlying villages as I am,' Edward lied glibly. 'I have no doubt that the woman has fled back to her usual haunts, and were I to go in search of her I would be recognised by those who give her sanctuary. Barton, on the other hand, can ride through the countryside in search of her without arousing suspicion.'

'Whatever the excuse, and wherever she may currently be,' Kincaid said with a sour expression, 'there can be no public trial on the morrow, as we had planned.'

'Unless Bailiff Barton can locate her before tomorrow morning,' Edward suggested, to a howl from Byron.

'And *that* is as likely as my walking on the surface of the Trent! You have proved yourself both incompetent and dishonest, Mountsorrel, and you are no longer my bailiff! Thanks to your dishonesty — and for whatever reason, I choose not to conjecture — a dangerous prisoner — a witch, no less — has broken loose. She is no doubt roaming my estate, bringing curses down on the heads of those who serve me with loyalty, poisoning my cattle, souring my crops and perhaps even raising the spirit of the Black Monk to further terrify my estate workers.'

'You suspect that I was complicit in the woman's escape?' Edward asked in what he intended to be a tone of disbelief, but now that Byron was in full stride there was no stopping him.

'I suspect that _you_ are also a witch!' he screamed as he backed away towards the doorway and called loudly for the turnkey. 'Those who follow Satan's path are not all women — they've been known to draw men into their net of wickedness, too. Tomorrow was set aside for the testing of a witch, and test a witch we shall! You are to be confined, on pain of death to anyone who seeks to conspire in your release. Turnkey, secure his hands and feet, and take him below!'

Edward rapidly came to realise how much respect his Shire Hall colleagues had for him. While they could not ignore the demand from Sheriff Byron that Edward be locked away while awaiting trial for witchcraft the following morning, they were nevertheless both distressed and embarrassed at having to carry it out, and were determined to make life as comfortable as possible for him. Not only was he brought adequate food and drink, but he was also allocated a cell just below ground level, where the air was sweeter thanks to an open grille at the top, where the ceiling of the cell came level with the yard into which prisoners were occasionally marched in order to be counted, or for their cells to be cleaned in a rudimentary fashion.

It was through this grille that his own men took it in turns to communicate with him, continually offering their apologies for what they had been required to do, and offering him beer, bread and cheese. They even contrived to visit the pie vendor in Weekday Cross, and as the clock on the spire of St Mary's tolled the doleful hour of midnight two mutton pies were handed down through the grille.

Edward was drifting into an uneasy sleep when he heard what sounded like the word of God coming down to him from the heavens, although the sentiment it expressed was neither holy nor consoling.

'Lying down on the job as usual, Mountsorrel, while I do everything for you?'

He opened his eyes blearily and gazed up through the grille, where a bulky shape was blocking out the faint glow from the moon.

'Either that's God seeking to chastise me for past sins, or it's Francis Barton urging me to commit more,' he said with a chuckle. 'Either way, you're too late for the meat pies, and you should be advised that you're at considerable risk of being deprived of the office of bailiff to the Sheriff of Nottingham.'

'At least I'm not locked inside one of my own cells,' Francis mocked him. 'They tell me that was on Byron's orders — what did you do, tell him the truth about his ugly face?'

'No, he finally learned that Rose is not confined down here, awaiting her trial as a witch on the morrow. Instead he's planning on trying me for the same offence.'

'He should have awaited my return,' Francis said with a laugh.

Edward tutted. 'So that you could explain to him why she isn't locked away awaiting trial?'

'I imagine that you've already attempted that, hence your presence down there. But she *will* be available for trial.'

'Don't jest with me, Francis — I'm not in the mood.'

'I don't jest, Edward. She'll be there at ten of the forenoon, along with me and Kitty.'

'You found her?'

'No, she found us. We spent days scouring every known refuge that she might have sought, and I seem to have met every cousin, aunt, nephew, niece and old friend of Rose Middleham that ever existed. Then late last night there was a knock on the shutter of Kitty's bedchamber and a demand for elderberry wine that we were only too glad to accommodate.'

'She returned home voluntarily?'

'She did indeed, with some story about you being in danger. How she knew what Byron was planning I have no idea.'

'She has the second sight, remember? She must have read Byron's mind.'

'She also seemed to know that there was a trial scheduled for tomorrow morning, and she insisted that she be brought back to Nottingham to answer for her actions, prove that she is no witch, and save your sorry arse from further punishment.'

'A truly remarkable lady in many ways,' Edward replied as his hopes soared, before he reminded himself of the obstacles, lies and sheer blind prejudice that Rose would need to overcome if she was to retain her freedom, and even her life.

'You must tell her not to expose herself to danger on my account,' Edward urged Francis. 'She is to be applauded for her courage, but I am in a better position to argue my innocence.'

'She certainly doesn't lack courage,' Francis agreed, 'but neither can she be dissuaded from her chosen course, once she has settled on it. I might also add that her sister is even worse, and that she has formed the opinion that she should become Mistress Barton.'

Edward laughed out loud despite the perilous position in which he found himself. 'I *knew* that this would happen someday. You've tupped one widow too many, Francis Barton, and now your sins have found you out. Elizabeth will be delighted.'

'Is she still in Ashby with the children? And do you wish me to get word to her of your current plight?'

'For God's sake, no!' Edward pleaded. 'She would only tell you that this is all my own fault.'

'You underestimate her love for you,' Francis told him. 'I have seen the devotion that exists between you, as might anyone with healthy eyesight. In fact, the pleasure I've derived from watching Edward Mountsorrel surrounded by his loving family has half inclined me towards matrimony.'

'Well, the other half of you had better get off that cold ground and set about protecting Rose and Kitty,' Edward told him. 'Where do you have them hidden?'

'My house. Where else?'

'Isn't that where Sheriff Byron and his witch-finder would think to look first?'

'They already have,' Francis said with a chuckle, 'and Ralph proved his worth by pretending that Rose was his aunt, and that Kitty was her guardian.'

'Guardian?' Edward echoed, to a guffaw from Francis.

'Yes, the guardian of Ralph's "Mad Aunt Bessie". Rose made a wonderful show of foaming at the mouth, and Byron couldn't leave fast enough.'

Edward burst out laughing, then reminded himself that levity was hardly appropriate in his circumstances.

'So you will attend here at the Shire Hall on the morrow, with Rose?'

'I will indeed,' Francis confirmed, 'and you'll owe me so many mutton pies that I'll burst out of my hose after eating them.'

14

The turnkeys came for Edward an hour after sunrise, apologising with red faces and downcast eyes as they led him up the stairs and into a corridor within the Shire Hall that he knew well from escorting prisoners to their fate at the county assizes, but had never expected to travel himself.

A door was pulled open, revealing a short set of stairs that led upwards. The noise from an expectant crowd immediately assailed his ears, and he took a deep breath as he appeared in the dock that occupied the central spot in the old courtroom. There were some catcalls, but not as many as might normally be expected when a prisoner made his first appearance, because most of those who had gathered to watch the spectacle of a man on trial knew who he was, and some of them had cause to be grateful for his forbearance in the past.

'We'll keep the chains loose, sir,' one of the turnkeys told him almost apologetically, 'but we've got our jobs to do, and we has to make it look like we've got you secure. Please don't make a run for it, else we'll be in trouble.'

'Have no fear of that,' Edward reassured the turnkey, who was in the process of taking the chains that ran from their ankle mountings around Edward's boots and fixing them to the bolts on either side of the dock that would hold Edward secure during the proceedings. Edward's wrists were also in chains, but whether by design or oversight the turnkey omitted to link them together. By keeping his hands still, Edward could give the appearance of being manacled at the wrists.

The court tipstaff called for silence, and when there was no obvious diminution in the noise created by two hundred men talking among themselves and speculating on the likely outcome, the court official banged his staff of office three times on the wooden floor and bellowed, 'Silence on pain of imprisonment! Hear the word of lawful authority and be still!'

The hubbub died sufficiently for the worthy official to shout at the top of his voice, 'Pray silence for the High Sheriff of Nottinghamshire!' A door at the rear of the raised bench opened, and in walked Sheriff Byron, attended by several men at arms carrying halberds, and followed by John Kincaid. They took their seats on the bench, while the attendants fanned out to form a largely ceremonial guard in front of them. The tipstaff then called, 'This honourable court is now in session. God save the queen!'

Byron looked across at the man who had served him faithfully as his bailiff for the best part of a year as he called out, 'Master Clerk, please read the charge to the prisoner and take his plea in response.'

Edward was gently urged to his feet as a man rose from across the courtroom, lifted a single sheet of vellum to eye level, adjusted an eyeglass with his other hand, and read the accusation against Edward.

'Edward Mountsorrel, formerly bailiff to the High Sheriff of Nottinghamshire, and now charged in your capacity as a resident of Whitefriars Lane within the parish of St Nicholas and the jurisdiction of the town of Nottingham, that on diverse dates in this year of our Lord 1596, and the thirty-eighth year of the reign of our sovereign and most gracious majesty Queen Elizabeth, within the town of Nottingham aforesaid, you did wantonly, willingly and with malice aforethought consort with a witch. How say you, Edward Mountsorrel, be ye guilty or not guilty?'

'I cannot plead one way or the other to such a defective charge,' Edward replied in a clear voice that rang commandingly across the courtroom.

'How say you that the charge is defective?' Byron demanded with obvious irritation.

Edward smiled back confidently as he pointed out, 'You do not name the witch. And you do not *produce* any witch. How can I know how to plead in the absence of such essentials? There is also the matter of jurisdiction. You are the sheriff of the county, and yet it is alleged that my offence occurred here in the town. Apart from that, should I not be arraigned before an Assize Court or perhaps a Quarter Session? Where is your authority to preside over this proceeding?'

'As for my jurisdiction,' Byron spat back in reply, 'I am commissioned by Her Majesty to preserve the peace for the county, as you would appear to concede, and the witch in question was residing within the county before you were prevailed upon — for reasons that shall hopefully emerge — to afford her safe conduct into the town, where you connived at her release. This brings the matter within the remit of my jurisdiction.'

'Even if that be the case,' Edward responded, 'where is your witch?'

'I am here, but I am no witch,' came a woman's voice from the back of the courtroom. The crowd parted like ripples in a pond into which a stone had been thrown, revealing Rose, with Francis on one side of her and Kitty on the other.

Byron smiled broadly as he called out, 'Have the witch brought into the well of the court.'

'I am no witch,' Rose repeated as one of the constables who had entered the courtroom in company with Francis led her towards the table under the raised bench.

'You are known as Magic Mary?' Byron asked.

She bowed her head serenely. 'There are some who call me that,' she conceded. 'My true name is Rose Middleham, but under neither name am I a witch.'

'Place her in the dock along with the other prisoner,' Byron commanded. The turnkey opened the front flap in order to allow her to enter the dock and take a seat beside Edward, who smiled warmly. He watched the turnkey wrap manacles around Rose's ankles and wrists and then pass a chain through them that was bolted to the floor.

'You should not have come here today,' Edward admonished her gently.

'I could not let you be accused of what amounted to nothing more than kindness.'

'You know that I am accused of consorting with a witch?'

'I knew that you had been apprehended and charged with something, but I knew not what precisely.'

'How did you know even that?'

'Did I not tell you that I have the second sight? I was staying with an old friend who's married to the farrier in Southwell village, but returned to Daybrook and asked that I be brought here. By the way, I believe that your friend Francis may shortly become my brother-in-law.'

'It's to be hoped, since he really needs a wife and family, and he's not getting any younger.'

'Be that as it may,' Rose said, 'if Kitty is to be believed, he does not lack vigour.'

'The two prisoners will remain silent until spoken to!' Byron bellowed from the bench, causing them both to fall silent. He turned to address the crowd. 'As the prisoner Mountsorrel reminded us, the key to the charges faced by both prisoners is that of proving the woman to be a witch. Is there any person here who can give evidence of that?' The courtroom fell silent for a moment, but the expression of quiet confidence on Byron's face suggested that his enquiry had not been speculative.

'I most certainly can!' came a voice from the back of the courtroom, and a raggedly dressed woman stepped forward. 'I lived in Papplewick for many years, and before that in Linby, and I've seen many examples of this woman conniving with the Devil to further her evil schemes.'

'That's Agnes Merryweather,' Rose whispered to Edward out of the corner of her mouth. 'The one who tried to steal Kitty's husband, remember?'

'I remember,' Edward replied, 'and it would seem that she's out for revenge.'

'Step forward, state your name, and then give your testimony,' Byron commanded.

Agnes stepped forward with a malicious gleam in her eye. 'My name is Agnes Merryweather, and I have seen cattle die in the fields after this woman —' she pointed at Rose in the dock — 'cast the evil eye over them.'

'Fields in which water hemlock might be found?' Edward shouted back defiantly. 'A root that is fatal to cattle if they are allowed to graze on it? And you must have been there also, to have seen it, so why might it not have been *your* evil eye that caused their deaths?'

'Silence!' Byron thundered. 'You have no right to question this witness!'

'I most certainly do,' Edward insisted. 'I am on trial accused of consorting with a witch, which gives me the right to challenge the evidence being given to prove that the woman accused alongside me is a witch. Go ahead, Mistress

Merryweather — answer my challenge: could the cattle to which you refer have died by eating plants fatal to them?'

'A dog on the Newstead estate was found with its throat ripped out!' Agnes insisted, ignoring Edward's challenge.

'Are you suggesting that Mistress Middleham did that with her own bare teeth?' Edward demanded, to a responding ripple of laughter through the crowd.

'Of course not,' Agnes snapped as she reddened slightly. 'She must have done so in the guise of her familiar — perhaps a wolf. If she's a witch, then she'll have a familiar.'

'Let me see if I understand what you're alleging,' Edward replied, as Byron seemed to abandon any attempt to silence him. 'You say that one sign that she's a witch is that a dog was found with its throat ripped out. But she could only have done that by means of her familiar — a familiar that presumably you've never seen — and from this it may be concluded that she's a witch? I have a four-year-old daughter who could see through the mangled logic of that. You seek to prove that she's a witch by assuming that she must be!'

'I saw a wolf in the trees above the Newstead estate once!' Agnes persisted.

'And I once saw a creature they call a lion, in the animal enclosure at the Tower of London when I was posted there as a soldier,' Edward replied. 'That doesn't mean that it attacked Sheriff Byron's dog, does it? And how do you know that it wasn't in fact a real wolf? If you can't prove that, then how can you now allege that it must have been Rose Middleham's familiar?'

'She once sold amulets to workmen engaged in repairs to Newstead Hall, to ward off the ghost of the Black Monk!' Agnes shouted in mounting desperation.

'And did they prevent this ghost from appearing?' Edward challenged her.

This time, Byron could not resist shouting, 'No, they did not!'

'That proves my point, I think,' Edward said with a triumphant smile. 'Had this lady been a real witch, the ghostly visitations would have ceased!'

Agnes was still searching her mind for some other allegation to throw at Rose when Kincaid leant towards Byron and muttered something in his ear, to which Byron nodded. Edward seized this moment of inattention from the bench to whisper to Rose, 'I need to speak with Francis urgently!'

Rose dipped her head in understanding, then suddenly fell to one side as if in a faint. She was too tightly restrained to fall completely, but hung limply by her manacled wrists.

Edward feigned concern as he called out, 'Mistress Middleham is clearly distressed by all these accusations — can someone come to her assistance?'

'I'm her sister!' Kitty called as she rushed forward, accompanied by Francis.

As they fussed over her, Rose whispered, 'Edward needs to speak to Francis.' Francis made a show of leaning into the dock to prop Rose upright, and Edward whispered in his ear. Francis looked surprised, but nodded his agreement, then stood back.

'May we please continue?' Byron demanded as Rose appeared to be revived, clearly lacking any sympathy for her.

Edward continued his attack on Agnes. 'Who are you to be telling this court how to recognise a witch? Do you have experience of your own?'

'Of course not!' Agnes protested. 'I'm merely here to tell what I know of Rose Middleham's wicked ways.'

'And what of her sister Catherine?' Edward asked. 'Is *she* a witch as well?'

'What has this to do with the matter in hand?' asked Byron. 'Cease these meaningless questions immediately, or I'll have you taken below!'

'And deny an accused person the right to defend himself?' Edward replied. 'That would hardly endear you to the Lord Chief Justice, Sir John Popham, would it? A very good friend of *your* very good friend Sheriff Kniveton, or so he assured me only recently.'

Byron appeared to pale somewhat, and had nothing to say in response other than, 'Continue — but keep it relevant to the matter in hand.'

'Certainly,' Edward said, then turned to face Agnes. 'You and the Middleham sisters have been sworn enemies for many years, have you not?'

'What do you mean?' Agnes replied defiantly. 'We were neighbours in Linby many years ago, certainly, but that was all.'

'And during that time you took it upon yourself to cast a spell on a certain young man who was betrothed to Catherine Middleham, did you not?'

'And who might that be?' Agnes challenged him.

'His name was Thomas Fellows. Remember him? He eventually married Catherine Middleham once the spell you had cast on him fell away from his eyes.'

'I cast no spell on him, but there was certainly a time when he seemed to wander in his affections from Catherine to me.'

'Ensnared by your natural beauty, no doubt,' Edward suggested, to roars of appreciative laughter from the crowd.

'That's enough!' Byron yelled down. 'You cannot complain of any lack of opportunity to ask questions in your own defence, Mountsorrel, but those last have no relevance to the question before the court, which is whether or not Rose Middleham is a witch. Do you have any further *meaningful* questions?'

'Just one,' Edward replied calmly as he looked towards Francis. On a whispered instruction from Francis, two constables moved stealthily behind Agnes, who appeared not to notice as she glared back at Edward.

'You haven't always sought to appear beautiful, have you?' Edward said accusingly. 'In fact, on one very significant day in the recent past, you went out of your way to look menacing, did you not?'

'Your meaning?' she challenged him.

Edward's hands appeared to break free from his shackles as his arm shot out to point an accusing finger in Agnes's direction. 'My meaning is this! Less than two weeks ago, we hanged a man named Amos Hutchins at Gallows Hill. No sooner had he choked his final breath than a woman leapt onto the cart that had brought him there and cursed the gallows, and all of those in attendance at the hanging. Since then there have been nightly visitations of the souls of the dead, threats of demonic curses being cast upon the town, and other such machinations worthy of theatrical players at their most devious. Yet not a single living soul in Nottingham has so far perished by demonic means, and not a single witch, demon, ghost or devil has been seen in its streets. We might ask ourselves why, but you know *precisely* why, do you not, Mistress Merryweather? *You* were that so-called witch!'

'How can you accuse me of such wickedness?' Agnes demanded as she stepped backwards into the arms of Francis's constables.

'I can because I was there, and I recognised you as soon as you stepped forward in this courtroom,' replied Edward. 'You have, I fear, rather cooked your own goose by being so eager to testify against your old adversary Rose Middleham, who never did harm to anyone. Indeed, there are many who could attest to her good works, and the blessings she has bestowed upon others through her knowledge of natural physick.'

'She cured my boils!' came a man's voice from the back.

'My wife was in terrible pain, but Magic Mary shifted it!' called another.

'She delivered my five babies!' a woman yelled from somewhere down the side.

'All through witchcraft, no doubt!' Byron called out. 'A witch can do good things as well as bad, in order to obscure their true purpose.'

'A good person can also do good things out of love!' Rose yelled back, incensed, before Byron demanded that she remain silent.

He turned his glare on Edward. 'You accuse Agnes Merryweather — who has bravely come forward to testify — of being a witch herself?'

'No. I accuse her of *pretending* to be a witch!' Edward retorted. 'Take her below!'

'You forget that you are no longer the county bailiff!'

Francis moved forward. 'This is Nottingham, not the county, and a woman has been accused of practising dishonesty at a hanging conducted under my supervision. I'm still bailiff to the Sheriff of Nottingham — *both* of them — and this woman is coming below with me. Take her down, boys!'

Agnes struggled and blasphemed as two pairs of brawny arms lifted her clean off her feet and carried her out through the door of the courtroom that led to the cells. There were jeers and catcalls from the assembled throng, and John Kincaid leapt to his feet as he shouted for order. Byron hammered on his bench with a gavel, and the court gradually fell silent, allowing Kincaid to be heard above the general hubbub.

'We have no need of witness testimony in this matter, either for or against the accused. There is one simple test that I have never known to fail. Let the woman Middleham be brought into the well of the court, where I will administer the pricking tool. *Then* we shall see who is the witch!'

15

'Do you *really* think I'm a witch?' Rose asked Edward fearfully.

'Of course I don't,' Edward assured her. 'But that man Kincaid, who's sitting alongside Byron, is about to prove that you are. Have no fear; I know how the trick is performed and I can prove your innocence. But you'll have to forgive me in advance for inflicting brief pain on you.'

Rose shuddered. 'I'll be guided by you.'

'Bring Mistress Middleham forward!' Kincaid commanded. He extracted a round metal object from his tunic and left the bench, to stand before Rose as Francis led her gently forward, with Kitty, as ever, close beside him.

'Hold out your arm, and roll the sleeve of your gown back to the elbow,' Kincaid instructed Rose, who duly obliged. Then Kincaid called out for the benefit of everyone in the courtroom, 'I have never known this method to fail in unmasking witches and wizards.' He held up the metal instrument, from which a two-inch long spike could clearly be seen protruding.

'If she be a witch, her master the Devil will protect her, and when I plunge this sharp point into her flesh there will be no wound. If she bleeds, she is innocent. So, let us call upon those beyond the veil of our perception to be the judge.'

Rose held out her arm and closed her eyes in anticipation as Kincaid made a stabbing motion with the device. He then gave a yell of triumph and held up the pricking tool to public view.

'Behold! There is no blood because the wretch has been protected by her Dark Lord the Devil. Let us waste no further time in taking this woman out to be executed!'

'Halt!' thundered Edward.

Kincaid glared at him. 'What further foolishness do you seek to engage in? The woman is a witch, and she must die!'

'Whatever skill you may possess in unmasking witches — which is very little — you clearly do not know the law in this country, whatever it may be in your native Scotland. Under a statute proclaimed by Her Majesty Queen Elizabeth some years ago, a witch may only be put to death if her evil has led to the death of some person. You have thus far produced no evidence of same, and I suggest that none exists. And in any case she is no witch, as I shall demonstrate, if you would hand over your instrument of trickery.'

'It will only work in my hand,' Kincaid objected, the fear evident in his eyes.

'If the outcome of the ordeal is indeed ordained by the Devil, then it should not matter who has the instrument in their hand. So I ask again — hand it over to me.'

'No!' Kincaid insisted.

Edward thought quickly. He looked up to where Byron was watching the proceedings with a puzzled expression and called out, 'Sheriff Byron, you suggested earlier in these proceedings that I might be a witch myself — do you not wish your chosen witch-finder to test the device on me? Or are you fearful that such a process would only serve to prove my innocence?'

Byron and Kincaid exchanged an uneasy glance before Byron nodded. 'It shall be as you suggest. Proceed with the ordeal, Master Kincaid.'

With a sour smirk Kincaid pulled back Edward's tunic sleeve and held the device high in the air. As the spike came down rapidly towards him, Edward instinctively flinched, in case Kincaid was sufficiently incensed by his effrontery to wish to cause him pain. Fortunately, there was only a faint clicking noise, audible only to the two men, as the device landed on Edward's arm with sufficient force to cause a bruise.

'See!' Kincaid yelled. 'Two witches in one morning! God be praised, and the Devil be cursed back to his evil pit!'

In the process of casting a gloat of triumph towards the assembled throng Kincaid committed the elementary error of loosening his grip on his device, which Edward grabbed in one swift motion. It took everyone by surprise, no doubt having forgotten the earlier incident in which he had demonstrated that his wrists were not manacled. Kincaid gave a howl of rage and demanded, 'Give that back immediately!'

'Not until I have proved the innocence of two people!' Edward said as he took a step backwards, found the switch on the side of the device that he had been praying actually existed, and pressed it down, hoping that the spike would remain in position when he gritted his teeth and rammed it into his own bare arm.

There was a collective gasp from the crowd as a spurt of blood shot from Edward's forearm. Then he turned to Rose and apologised before stabbing her in the arm, drawing blood and causing her to whimper in pain.

'How can this be?' he demanded rhetorically as he held up the blood-stained spike for public scrutiny. 'One minute we are witches, and the next minute we are not. Has the Devil fallen asleep? Does Satan play games with us? Or is this simple trickery on the part of a mountebank who rightly belongs with a troupe of travelling players, selling "cure-all" potions? Would anyone else care to be tested for their standing as a witch? I can either confirm you as one, or declare your innocence, as I deem appropriate. And how may I achieve this miracle, you ask? Behold!'

He held the tool high in the air and retracted the spike. 'Now you're a witch,' he called, before flicking the side switch and allowing the spike to click out and remain in place. 'Now you're not.'

A rumble of disapproval became audible, but it was not directed against Edward. A leather shoe flew through the air and hit Kincaid on the side of the head as someone called out, 'Villain! Scoundrel! Sharper!'

Taking advantage of the prevailing mood, Edward cried out, 'How many innocent souls have you put to death using this trickery, Master Kincaid? Should it not be you on trial yourself — for *murder*?'

Kincaid opted not to remain and debate the point, instead scurrying hastily back onto the Bench, from which he and Byron disappeared by way of the back door as more missiles sailed in their direction. Francis called for order, but made no effort to chase after the two retreating men. Instead, while uproar reigned in the courtroom he ordered that Edward and Rose be freed from their shackles, a task achieved in record time by the grinning turnkeys. Kitty and Rose embraced, and Rose looked over her sister's shoulder to mouth a silent *thank you* to Edward, who nodded back.

'You dealt with that very well,' Francis congratulated Edward, 'but I must own that I would never have recognised that Merryweather woman as the old crone at the hanging.'

'I got a better look at her from the front,' Edward explained, 'but I look forward to learning who put her up to it.'

'You must be hungry,' Francis observed. 'Come home with me and let's see what Ralph can rummage up for us.'

'No more meat pies,' Edward said. 'My men kept me well supplied with those last night. But I would welcome a chance to wash.'

'I was hoping you'd say that,' Francis said, as he led the way out through the rapidly emptying courtroom. 'You smell particularly ripe after a night in the cells.'

Two days later they'd taken all the necessary steps to move their enquiries on, and to report back what they knew to those who needed to know. Their first visit after breakfast had been to Sheriff Stokely, who smiled with pleasure as the two men recounted the precise circumstances in which Kincaid had been unmasked as a fraud.

'I hear that Byron has beaten a hasty retreat to Newstead,' said Stokely, 'and when I called on Sheriff Kniveton I was advised that he was confined with a fever. But not so confined that he couldn't peer at me through his shutter as I was leaving. I believe that he and Byron are very worried men at present.'

'What will happen to them?' Edward asked.

Stokely shrugged. 'That will depend upon Matthew Parkin when I get word back to him in Ashby. Or perhaps the decision will be made in London, when he in turn reports back to Cecil. For the time being you must concentrate all your efforts on learning the truth about what's been going on at Gallows Hill.'

'Francis will need to take charge of that,' Edward pointed out, 'since I was dismissed from office by Sheriff Byron.'

Stokely smiled. 'There may well be another sheriff in place once news reaches London regarding Byron's appalling complicity in those farcical scenes in the Shire Hall. However, in the absence of any formal bailiff appointment, which may well fall to the next county sheriff as his first task, you may work alongside Barton, and I'll make arrangements for you to be remunerated as a senior constable. It will be better than nothing.'

'What about Kincaid?' Edward asked, and this time Stokely laughed out loud.

'Last heard of creating dust clouds somewhere north of Doncaster on his way back to Scotland. That just leaves Kniveton.'

'Can he be implicated in Byron's misdeeds?' Francis asked eagerly.

'That may depend upon what you discover when you reveal the trickery at Gallows Hill. If there's any evidence that he encouraged sleight of hand and other dissimulation up here, then he too will be leaving his office long before it is due to expire. As you'll be aware, we were both appointed for a year, and that terminates in March of next year. So what witnesses do you have who may be of assistance?'

'Before I was arrested and thrown into my own cells,' Edward explained, 'I ordered the removal down into the Shire Hall cells of a man named Henry Burridge, a strolling player apprehended in Newark when members of his band began prostituting themselves in the back yard of a local alehouse. I intend to offer to reduce those charges that I deliberately inflated in exchange for his advising us how Agnes Merryweather succeeded in disappearing in broad daylight after playing the role of the witch at the hanging of Amos Hutchins. She will hopefully be prepared to give up Byron and the others.'

'Much though I would like to see Byron hauled before the court,' Stokely said ruefully, 'I believe you will learn that he was the dupe of others. Others with connections to a certain estate in Derbyshire, who no doubt leaned on him to make as much as he could of the suspicion of witchcraft in Nottinghamshire. Likewise Kniveton, who is stupid enough to actually believe all the superstitious gong spouted by Robert Aldridge from his pulpit in St Mary's. But good luck in your investigations, anyway.'

'Where should we begin?' Francis asked Edward as they sat burning their mouths with freshly baked mutton pies in the churchyard of St Mary's later that day. 'And don't think for one moment that I shall accept the leading role in this investigation, just because you're no longer a bailiff. In fact, you can have my office if you wish, since my interest is now more in apple farming.'

'Did Rose and Kitty get home safely?' Edward asked.

Francis nodded. 'I took them back late yesterday, while you were at home catching up on your sleep. Rose was singing your praises all the way. I think she wants you to be made a saint.'

'I was just glad to be able to expose that witchcraft nonsense for what it is. And hopefully we can do the same with regard to that buffoonery at Gallows Hill, so no more talk of you spending your days harvesting apples.'

'It may be what I am destined to do,' Francis remarked quietly.

Edward looked at him with raised eyebrows. 'Mistress Fellows has *really* engaged your attention for longer than a quick bedding? Both you and Rose suggested that she might have designs on becoming Mistress Barton. Tell me that you haven't changed your ways *that* easily.'

'I fear I may have,' Francis admitted, 'but let's talk of other things. For example, what are you still hiding from me regarding all this witchcraft and devilry that seems to have plagued us recently? Stokely suggested, and not for the first time, that it may be part of something deeper, and he made reference to Matthew Parkin. Wasn't he the man you went to see in Ashby? You must tell me the whole, if you intend to drag me into further investigation at Gallows Hill.'

Edward sighed. 'Where to begin? Bear in mind that even I don't have the entire background, and that Parkin proved to be typical of those who are close to the throne. He is very tight with his intelligence, hints at things rather than disclosing them fully, and wraps everything in a cloak of intrigue that cannot be removed because it concerns the Crown.'

'But you still have knowledge that I don't?' Francis asked.

'I do. It would seem that there is still uncertainty over who will inherit Elizabeth's throne upon her passing, and you may recall that there is one group of influential courtiers who favour a Catholic successor. That was why we were sent into Leicestershire that time, of course, and hopefully the name Arbella Stuart still remains in your memory.'

'Indeed it does, but we put paid to that lot, surely?'

'Only some of them, it would seem, but there remain others who oppose the popular choice in Westminster, namely the passing of the English crown to King James of Scotland, principally because of his Protestant inclinations.'

'But what has this to do with…' Francis began, causing Edward to raise his hand for silence.

'As I was saying,' Edward continued, 'there are those who do not wish James to accept the English throne, and have embarked on a strategy to deter him from doing so. He is known to have an abhorrence of witchcraft, and therefore these people set about creating the impression that England is awash in it. By this means they hope that he will stay well north of the border. They were the ones who summoned that charlatan John Kincaid down here, to expose witches under every rock, on every riverbank and in every stretch of forest. *Now* do you understand?'

'Yes,' said Francis. 'And it is our appointed task to prove that it is all trumpery?'

'Precisely. It was Parkin who advised me of the false device with which Kincaid exposed innocent women as witches, and it must be assumed that he was being paid handsomely for every one that he discovered. He is presumably running back to Scotland as fast as his mount will carry him, and our remaining task is to prove that the events at Gallows Hill came from the same stable of untruths and false display.'

'And how do you propose that we do that?'

'As I mentioned when we spoke with Stokely, I have a man called Henry Burridge in the cells below the Shire Hall. I suggest that we have him transferred to the meanest cell under the Guildhall, where he comes under your lawful custody. He will not have learned that I am no longer the county bailiff, but I will enlist his assistance, as a term of his release, in revealing to us how all those weird nightly goings-on at Gallows Hill might have been achieved. In fact, I propose that we take him with us when we journey up there again, this time by day.'

'But what of Agnes Merryweather? She is also in the Guildhall cells, and thanks to your eagle eye we now know that she was the so-called witch who called down the powers of darkness in the first place. Will she admit to that, do you think?'

'There's only one way to find out,' replied Edward, 'so let us set about it before the day progresses further.'

Agnes Merryweather made no effort to rise from the damp corner of the windowless, airless cell in which she was crouched as Edward and Francis entered.

'I have only one thing to say,' she croaked, 'and that is to curse the pair of you. You will twist and turn in the agony of the fires of Hell, never to be released from the torment!'

'You will notice, if you look carefully,' Edward replied with heavy sarcasm, 'that my knees are not knocking in fear. You are no more a witch than I am a milkmaid. But if anyone is cursed, it's you. Cursed to burn in the funeral pyre at Smithfield, which is the fate that awaits all females convicted of high treason.'

Agnes threw her head back in defiance. 'I committed no treason, high or otherwise. I simply did as I was asked, and gave a rather apt performance as a witch. I should perhaps be part of a group of strolling players.'

'Perhaps that would have been preferable to posing as a witch all these years,' Edward agreed. 'Your downfall was seeking to ensnare Thomas Fellows, was it not? Then such powers that you might have possessed were taken from you, and you were reduced to a pretence.'

'There were still many who were prepared to pay handsomely for what they believed to be my powers,' she told them.

'So who paid you to leap onto a cart at the hanging of Amos Hutchins and pretend to curse all those in attendance?' Edward demanded.

'I will tell you only that he was no more capable of treason than I am of passing through the walls of this cell.'

'Perhaps not he,' Edward told her, 'but those who were paying *him*. You really have no idea of the web of intrigue in which you are enmeshed, like a fly at the mercy of the spider who wove it. It is *they* who tilt for the throne of England.'

'But I was not to know that, was I?' she protested.

Edward shook his head sadly. 'Did you not think to enquire *why* you were being required to give that performance?'

'I cared not, provided that I was paid what was agreed. In advance, since it was part of the arrangement that I would disappear swiftly from sight once I had pronounced the curse. Then I was invited back to give nightly performances.'

'And how exactly did you do that?' Francis asked.

Agnes looked at him disdainfully. 'The other dog speaks! The age of miracles is not truly past, then.'

'You would have to hope not,' Edward replied as they turned to leave, 'since nothing short of a miracle can preserve you from burning. In *this* world, not in Hell, although what fate awaits you down there I do not dare to contemplate.'

'You are determined to charge me with treason?' Agnes asked, no longer sounding quite so brave.

Edward turned back. 'I have considerable influence over the nature of any charge, as you will no doubt be aware. If I am to be able to satisfy those in London to whom I report that your only intention was to earn a few paltry shillings, then I need to be assured that you knew nothing about the broader plot, but were in truth commissioned by someone who you believed was only interested in creating an amusing diversion from a humdrum life. It *was* Thomas Gullen who paid you, wasn't it?'

Agnes nodded. 'Two shillings for each performance. It seemed like a God-given bargain at the time.'

'Trust me,' Edward replied as he banged on the cell door for the turnkey to open it, 'God had nothing to do with it. But you have saved your own neck, and will be charged only with creating a public nuisance, provided that you testify as to who put you up to it.'

Francis paused at the door. 'Tell us, Agnes, how did you manage to evade capture up at Gallows Hill?'

She looked up at him with a grim smile. 'Look for the trapdoor in the ground among the trees.'

16

Meg was smiling from the sheer pleasure of having two men to cook for, rather than taking a solitary supper in her chamber, and Edward and Francis were being treated to the best remains from the Mountsorrel larder as they sat discussing their next move.

'At least we now know who made it possible,' Francis said as he carved himself some more pickled pork to go with his warm manchet slice. 'It must have been easy with the hangman Gullen preparing the ground in advance.'

'I suspected him all along,' said Edward, 'and as I recall, I expressed my reservations about the story he wove us when we first accused him of not keeping watch on the nightly performances. The ghostly voice that accompanied the flaming skull was obviously Agnes Merryweather's, but the *real* question is who bought Gullen's loyalty. We can use Burridge to reveal how the trickery was achieved, but unless Gullen is prepared to peach on those who were no doubt paying handsomely for the use of his gallows site, then we have nothing valuable to report.'

'And we have to be *very* careful who we report our findings to,' Francis reminded him. 'Since you're no longer the county bailiff, you can't be expected to report back to Byron. Which is perhaps just as well, since you seem to suspect him of being the one behind the entire business.'

'Don't you?' Edward asked. 'It was Byron who was determined to find a witch on his estate, which suggests that he was part of the same group who wished to send a message back to King James that England was not a safe nation to rule.

And it was Byron who was giving Kincaid his freedom to go around accusing people of being witches.'

'Only Rose, surely?'

Edward shook his head. 'She was clearly meant to be only the first. What I can't be certain of is whether Byron was part of the broader plot aimed at James's possible succession, or is simply a superstitious old fool who's easily convinced of phantoms under the floorboards.'

'Perhaps Kniveton could reveal that,' Francis suggested. 'He and Byron are obviously very close, and I have to report to him equally alongside Stokely. I'll obviously let Stokely know everything that we know, but if we could somehow present Kniveton with our own version of events, contrived to make it sound as if we're highly suspicious of Byron, then it will almost certainly get back to him and we may learn something from the nature of his responding actions.'

'You're really quite devious in your methods once you get your mind off widows,' Edward said, grinning, just as Meg came through the door from the scullery.

'The mistress is back, Master, and it looks as if she got some fine gentleman to escort her home. I were putting out the empty hogshead for the brewer when I saw them dismounting from the wagon. Shall I set more places at board?'

'It would seem that you may have a rival for Elizabeth's affections,' Francis said with a smirk as the front door flew open and Margaret rushed in at her usual breakneck pace. She caught sight of Francis and threw herself at him with a joyful shout, leaving Edward to scoop up Robert and cuddle him warmly.

'How's my big man today?' he asked.

'He's wondering how long his father's likely to be remaining at home *this* time,' Elizabeth replied as she came through the

155

door next and embraced Edward, kissing him warmly. 'We missed you, and the gentleman who's been left to unhitch the horse from the wagon very kindly offered to escort us back here, along with two men at arms who've been left back at The Swan in Low Pavement. His name's Matthew Parkin, and I know that you've already met him because he told me the real reason for our trip to Ashby. I'm *very* proud of you.'

'What exactly did he tell you?' Edward asked, a little concerned that Elizabeth might have been given confidential information that might render her vulnerable to questioning by the wrong people.

'That you're secretly working to ensure that Queen Elizabeth has a successor worthy of the English crown,' she replied. 'I don't know how, or why, exactly, but that's what he told me. Is it true, and is Francis involved as well?'

'The answer to both questions is yes,' Edward replied, 'but you must all be hungry and thirsty. As you can see, Meg's emptied the larder for Francis and myself, but there's still a good amount left, so get the children seated and I'll go and bring Matthew inside.'

'Pardon my presumption,' said Parkin as he looked up from where he was rubbing down the horse in the stable entrance, 'but it's been so long since I got to do this for myself. In Westminster there are obviously stable hands who do this sort of thing, but I was raised on a large estate in Wiltshire, and as a boy I loved to be with the horses.'

'I know what you mean,' said Edward, 'since I too was employed on the land before I became a soldier, and then a bailiff. I came out to thank you for bringing my family safely back from Ashby, but I suspect that you have other business than that, particularly since I'm advised that you brought men at arms with you.'

Parkin smiled. 'In my line of business, I never travel without them. But I hear that there have been dramatic developments here in Nottingham, about which I require to be advised without delay. However, given the high stakes for which these games are being played, it might be better were none of your family to overhear what you have to tell me, and what instructions I carry from Cecil.'

Edward nodded back towards the house. 'You will of course be expected to take supper with us, and it would look suspicious if you did not. However, just across the way is the house of Francis Barton, the Nottingham bailiff. He is currently taking supper in my house, but given our somewhat cramped accommodation, and the fact that Francis lives alone, with a spare bedchamber, it would be perfectly natural for you to sleep there overnight.'

'He has no family?'

'Not yet, although that might be about to change. However, for the moment he has the obvious place for you to be accommodated, so if you would feign tiredness after you have eaten I will arrange to escort you to his house, and there we may all three discuss the state of those affairs on which we are engaged.'

'How much does Barton know already?' Parkin asked with a concerned frown.

'He has been working with me throughout this entire business, and knows all that I know. You may trust him implicitly, and we must both rely on his authority, since I was dismissed from my office by Sheriff Byron. Francis, however, is still employed by both sheriffs here in town — Kniveton and Stokely — although we have grounds for believing that Kniveton is in league with Byron, and that they may both be working on the orders of others.'

'We must clearly lose no time in sharing intelligence,' said Parkin, 'and I am more than ready for my supper, so let us away inside.'

Back inside the large all-purpose living space in Edward's house, Francis was being monopolised by little Margaret as she sat bouncing up and down on his knee and pretending that he was her horse, while Robert sat quietly in a corner, with his eyes glued on the door for his father's return. Elizabeth was busy supervising Meg as between them they gathered the remaining items from the larder and brought them to the table, but she turned and smiled as Edward came in with Parkin at his heels. He was introduced to Francis, and the two men shook hands as Margaret slid into the seat at board next to her precious 'Uncle Francis'. Parkin took the seat next to Edward as Elizabeth welcomed him to the table.

'What business has brought you to Nottingham, Master Parkin?' she asked. 'We spoke only of matters relating to your life at court on our ride back from Ashby — is your presence in our town court related?'

'In a very general sense, yes,' Parkin smiled blandly back at her. 'From time to time Her Majesty requires minor officials such as myself to tour the nation and be reassured that all bodes well for it. That is best achieved by meeting with the sheriffs, of which of course Nottingham has two. I intend to converse with them on the morrow. Then I shall journey to Newstead, to speak with Sheriff Byron.'

'I'm sure that Edward, as Sheriff Byron's bailiff, would be more than content to guide you up there and effect the introductions,' Elizabeth suggested.

'That won't be necessary,' Parkin replied diplomatically, 'since he and I are well acquainted. Unlike many sheriffs, Byron is a regular visitor to court.'

'There is also the consideration that I am no longer Byron's bailiff,' Edward confessed, since it seemed the most appropriate moment at which to make the doleful announcement. When Elizabeth's mouth flew open, he added hastily, 'But I *am* a senior constable under Francis's command, and the stipend is little less than I was already earning.'

'What did you do to earn your dismissal from Byron's service?' Elizabeth demanded. 'And how do you propose that we live down the public shame of it?'

'I think you'll soon discover that Edward is something of a local hero,' Francis interjected, 'since he was able to prevent a local wise woman being condemned as a witch.'

'I thought that the pair of you were supposed to be *suppressing* witchcraft, not *defending* it,' Elizabeth said with a pout.

'The woman was clearly innocent,' responded Edward, 'but we have also been able to expose the actions of others who are not. The harrowing scenes at Gallows Hill are at an end, and the woman responsible is safely under lock and key in the Guildhall, while the innocent woman is back at the home she shares with her sister in Daybrook. A sister who has taken a shine to Francis here, so you may soon get your wish and see Francis settled in matrimony.'

'I'm making no promises, mind,' Francis hastened to add, 'but she and I certainly seem to have a pleasing commonality of disposition. Her name is Catherine, but everyone who knows her calls her Kitty, the name she much prefers.'

'I dread to think how precisely you have come to know her,' Elizabeth muttered, 'but I'm consoled to know that perhaps you might be about to settle down, particularly since it would seem that you are better placed than ever to lead my husband astray, and urge him into dangerous situations. At least when he had responsibilities in the county he was able to disengage himself from your influence.'

Parkin feigned a yawn as he pushed back his dish and smiled gratefully at Elizabeth.

'I thank you most sincerely for the generosity of your hospitality and the quality of your table, Mistress Mountsorrel, but I fear that the journey from Ashby seems to have caught up with me, and I have yet to secure accommodation for the night.'

'Francis has a spare chamber,' Edward announced on cue, 'and I feel sure that he would be more than happy to accommodate an envoy of Her Majesty.'

'Not quite an envoy,' Parkin said, blushing modestly, 'but one who goes about her minor business with a gladsome heart. And if Master Barton would pardon my intrusion on his hospitality, I'd be more than content to rest my head under his roof.'

'That's decided then,' Edward announced without any attempt to consult Francis on the matter. 'If you've supped sufficiently, I'll walk over there with you both, and perhaps share a libation with you before we all take to our beds.'

'Your new status as my senior constable does not entitle you to invite visitors to my house,' Francis muttered as they walked across the rough track, before he turned to Parkin and announced, 'but *you* are most welcome, Master Parkin. I merely wished to record the fact that this does not constitute any sort of precedent.'

'There was a very good reason why we needed to speak outside the hearing of my family,' Edward told Francis as they sat around his dining table while Ralph began filling pots from the hogshead of strong beer in the scullery. 'Master Parkin is sent by Cecil, and you will recall that he and I met when I sought him out in Ashby at the request of Sheriff Stokely. He wishes to be advised of our progress in the matter of unmasking those who have sought to hold the community in thrall through fear of witches and demons, and no doubt he in turn will tell us how far the matter impinges on affairs at court.'

'You first,' Parkin invited them, 'since this will then establish how much I am free to disclose.'

'You will recall when we last met,' Edward began, 'that we were in the process of investigating two matters here in Nottingham and its surrounding neighbourhood that we were advised might have wider implications. The first was the persecution of a lady from Papplewick accused by Sheriff Byron of being a witch, which you in turn advised me might well be part of a broader plot to depict England as a nation of witchcraft and associated devilry. To that end he'd hosted a man from Scotland named John Kincaid, of whom you seem to have already had knowledge when we met in Ashby. I'm delighted to be able to advise you that Francis and I were able to expose Kincaid as a charlatan and save the life of Byron's innocent victim.'

Parkin nodded. 'This much I knew from a despatch from George Stokely that reached me the following day. I in turn alerted the constable of the castle here in Nottingham, with orders for Kincaid to be pursued north. I can advise you that he was overtaken in York, and confessed to having been offered ten golden sovereigns for every witch that he unmasked. He was then escorted back to Edinburgh by a small armed band that contained a messenger who was carrying a despatch from Cecil addressed to King James. That despatch revealed Kincaid's true nature, and assured His Majesty that there were no witches in England.'

'Did Kincaid reveal the identity of his paymaster?' Edward asked eagerly.

Parkin shook his head. 'It must have been someone in possession of considerable wealth, and in confidence I can advise you that Cecil suspects his great rival Robert Devereux of being behind it all.'

'The Earl of Essex, Elizabeth's favourite?' Edward asked, aghast.

'It is feared that he has ambitions of his own to be declared her heir, which is why he fawns upon her so shamelessly. She, poor dupe that she is, believes that it is through love of her, but those of us whose eyes are not half blinded by vanity can see the situation for what it is. What I have just confided must be kept in the strictest confidence, you understand, but it explains why Essex may have a motive for wishing to keep James from the succession. But what of your other matter — the devilish manifestations at the execution site?'

'As regards the recent events at Gallows Hill,' said Edward, 'we can report that they are at an end. This much we can advise you with confidence, but with regret we must also add that there is no clear indication of who may have been behind it all. We have the woman who started the entire travesty by posing as a witch, but she will admit only that she did so for reward given to her by the public hangman, Thomas Gullen. He occupies a cottage on the site, and was therefore well positioned to enable the nightly manifestations to occur. We have yet to confront Gullen with what we know, but I have a man in custody under the Shire Hall who is a travelling player by trade, and may well be able to show us how it was all achieved. The actual mechanics of it all, I mean.'

'Do you hope to learn from this man Gullen who was behind the entire business?' Parkin asked eagerly.

Edward shrugged. 'I have given some thought to that, as I believe that it might also be Sheriff Byron, but my first concern is to be able to prove to those in Nottingham who live in fear that it was all a masquerade.'

Parkin shook his head vigorously. 'You must venture much further than that, if necessary by applying torture to this man Gullen, since the unmasking of the entire plot may well depend on establishing a link between these events in Nottingham and a certain family estate in Derbyshire.'

'You referred to that also in Ashby,' Edward reminded him, 'but you were not more specific. However, both Francis and I are familiar with the name Arbella Stuart, as your master Robert Cecil could confirm.'

'He already has,' Parkin told them, 'which is why I am authorised to tell you more, in order that you will fully appreciate the importance of the investigations you have already commenced. How much do you recall of what you have already learned about the young lady in question?'

'Only that her parentage makes her a claimant to the English throne with an equal right to that of James of Scotland. They are cousins, are they not, since their fathers were brothers?'

'Correct,' Parkin confirmed. 'But that is as far as the similarity goes. Whereas James — as a young boy orphaned after his mother the Scots Mary was executed, and brought up under regents and tutors — was raised as a Protestant, Arbella Stuart is the last in a long line of ardent Catholics, and as such is the great hope of those who wish to see a monarch installed on the throne of England who will take our Church back under the wing of Rome. She is therefore a valuable pawn in a vast power game in which her grandmother seeks to add to her already impressive wealth and status.'

'Her *grandmother*?' Edward and Francis echoed simultaneously, and Parkin nodded.

'Indeed, her grandmother, the formidable Elizabeth Cavendish, who became Elizabeth Talbot, Countess of Shrewsbury, acquiring great wealth on the death of her husband, some of which she has converted into a magnificent residence in Derbyshire known as Hardwick Hall, on the site of her original birthplace. She is now known to all as Bess of Hardwick, and when Arbella's parents died, Bess took her under her wing and began grooming her for the Crown of England.'

'Clearly she has every motive for keeping that from James of Scotland,' Edward observed. 'So is it your contention that it is this Bess who is behind the nightly displays at Gallows Hill, designed to deter James from wishing to become our king?'

Parkin frowned. 'It's not entirely clear. It may well be that the initiative for what has been happening can be traced to her, but what if the true origin lies closer to the throne?'

When both men looked puzzled, Parkin lowered his voice, despite the fact that they were alone in the house, Ralph having returned to his quarters.

'There is a belief in Westminster that Essex may be seeking to enhance his claim to the throne by marrying Arbella. He is currently married, but he also has a mistress, and he's said to be the most handsome and dashing man at court by those who can judge these things. If he could charm Elizabeth into naming him as her heir, then marry someone with Arbella's pedigree, then his claim would be unassailable. Your task is to follow the chain of command upward from the initial source, this man Thomas Gullen. If necessary, we can have him taken down to London and put to the rack in the Tower until he reveals who was paying him.'

'We were intending merely to demonstrate that the ghostly visitations were mere mummery,' Edward explained uneasily. 'Say you that we must hand Gullen over to the royal torturer?'

'If it eases your conscience,' Parkin replied, 'you may simply hand him over to me, and I will make the necessary arrangements. I propose that you lose no further time, but make an early start on the morrow.'

'We are long overdue our beds anyway,' Edward conceded, 'so I bid you both a good night. Francis, be ready by daybreak.'

He walked back across to his own house and gingerly tested the front door. Someone had locked it securely, so he went down the side of the house into the rear garden, where he tried the scullery door that led to the back of the building. Meg had left it on the latch in such a way that it required only a slight jiggle with the mechanism that Edward had adjusted some time ago, and he was able to access the main house after securing the scullery door again so that only Meg could access it from outside in the morning.

Once in the upper chamber he sat down gingerly on the bolster in order to remove his boots, hoping not to wake either Elizabeth or the children, who were in the adjoining chamber. He slid into bed and was just congratulating himself on his success when a calm but determined voice on the adjoining pillow told him, 'I had hoped that after our lengthy parting, you might be eager to be reunited with me in bed. Obviously not, so I hope you have nightmares.'

17

Francis slipped out of his house before daybreak. He found Edward already waiting for him in front of his own house, horse's bridle in hand.

'We have a busy day ahead of us,' Edward reminded him, 'so I hope you breakfasted while managing not to wake your guest.'

'He was still snoring as I finished the leftover potage,' Francis said with a grimace. 'It will serve him right if there's nothing left for him, since his snoring kept me awake half the night. At least you were spared that, and there was no doubt a much more appetising selection of leftovers to choose from in your larder.'

'There was, but I didn't want to risk waking the children,' Edward frowned. 'Robert in particular is a light sleeper, and I didn't want him waking Margaret, because then their noisy play would have woken Elizabeth, and she's far from impressed that I'm reduced to being a mere senior constable under your command. Fortunately, our journey to the Shire Hall will take us past the pie vendor's stall.'

'Will they let you see Burridge, given that you're no longer the county bailiff?' Francis queried.

Edward smiled as he swung into the saddle. 'I'm not certain, but it won't matter anyway, since you'll be pretending to transfer him to the Guildhall. Come on, let's take advantage of the quiet streets.'

An hour and two mutton pies later, they stood on either side of a puzzled-looking Henry Burridge on the steps of the Shire Hall, looking down at the rapidly filling thoroughfare.

'Should I not be in restraints of some sort?' Burridge asked. 'And why am I being taken from one prison to another?'

'You're not,' Edward told him, 'provided that you agree to make use of your knowledge and experience of staging dramatic displays for the ignorant masses. If you do so to our satisfaction, then you will no longer be facing an appearance at the next Quarter Sessions regarding the disgraceful antics of the ladies in your company of travelling mountebanks. You will be released to return to Newark, or wherever your company may currently be disporting themselves on some village green.'

'That's the best thing I've heard for days,' Burridge said, smiling. 'So where are we going next?'

'To a place called Gallows Hill,' Francis replied, 'which, as its name suggests, is where we hang those condemned to death in the courts here in Nottingham. There have, in the past week or more, been manifestations of a ghostly and devilish nature that we now know to have been the work of actors such as yourself. What we require from you is an explanation of how such illusions were achieved. We know *who* was responsible, but we need to know *how* they did it, since they were not naturally gifted with either an actor's cunning or a philosopher's intelligence.'

'That is the easy part, for you,' Edward added. 'The difficult part will be walking the two or three miles uphill that will take us to Gallows Hill. Your legs will no doubt be stiff after your lengthy confinement, but we have no spare horse, and I feel sure that you will shrink from travelling in the condemned wagon.'

'Have no concern on that score,' said Burridge, 'for I am craving physical activity after several days in a cramped and dingy cell, and my natural constitution inclines me to vigorous exercise.'

As they made their way slowly along High Pavement, Edward and Francis were surprised to see Matthew Parkin walking towards them with a welcoming smile, followed by two men at arms whose facial expressions were not so genial. The two parties halted as they grew close to each other. Parkin broke the silence.

'I am on my way to visit Sheriff Stokely, and am advised that he resides in Stoney Street. Am I proceeding in the right direction?'

'Yes indeed,' Francis confirmed with a backward jerk of his thumb. 'It's the next street along, to the left after you pass St Mary's Church. Did my boy provide you with breakfast?'

'That is one of the reasons why I am calling on Sheriff Stokely. Your boy was asleep on the scullery floor when I went in search of sustenance. Had it been a palace scullery I might have kicked him awake, but in deference to my host I left him where he was.'

'Neither he nor I enjoyed much sleep,' Francis replied coldly, 'since someone in the house was snoring. I think you will find that Sheriff Stokely has a larder better equipped for an unexpected guest.'

'Presumably you have other reasons for meeting with him than the search for breakfast?' Edward asked.

Parkin nodded. 'Indeed I do, but they must remain undisclosed until your return from what I suspect is your further investigation of this gallows site. Is the man with you the one you had in custody, and should you not have him more securely tied?'

'It's a long walk to Gallows Hill,' Edward replied, 'as he is about to discover. But should you wish to loan us the services of one of your armed attendants, he might prove persuasive regarding the information we wish to obtain from the hangman who lives there, as well as ensuring that Master Burridge here does not take flight on the way.'

Parkin gave instructions to one of the men at arms, whom he addressed as 'Giles', then wished Edward and Francis good luck in their investigations.

'When you have completed them, return to me at Stokely's house. Our discussions are likely to occupy most of the morning, and he also will be entitled to learn of your findings.'

They reached Gallows Hill in bright morning sunlight, and were met by a wary-looking Thomas Gullen as he stepped out of his cottage with a slice of bread and dripping in his hand.

'I weren't told about no hanging today,' he grumbled. 'And where's your wagon?'

'We aren't here to string anyone up — except perhaps your good self,' Edward said as Giles moved out from behind the group and stood next to Gullen with a drawn sword.

'What d'you reckon *I've* been up to?' Gullen demanded.

'We *know* what you've been up to,' Francis replied. 'The only remaining question is whether or not we have to torture the truth out of you.'

'About what?' asked Gullen, wide-eyed with fear. 'If you mean that there hole in the ground up there, you can ask Sheriff Kniveton about that, 'cos it were him what told me to show the workmen where to put it.'

'So you'll have no difficulty showing *us* where you put it, will you?' Edward said, and Gullen shook his head.

'Follow me, Masters,' he said as he made to walk away from the cottage door. He was grabbed by the arm by Giles.

'Release him, Giles,' said Edward, 'at least for long enough for him to show us his handiwork.'

'Not mine, you understand,' Gullen whined. 'It were blokes what was sent by Sheriff Kniveton, and he said as how it were

169

going to be a new place to drop them what's sent up here to be hung.'

'A hole in the ground?' Edward asked.

Gullen nodded. 'Over in them trees. I'll show you.'

They all walked across the path, under the permanent gallows, and into the copse of trees on the far side. Gullen was only too eager to assist, and walked swiftly to a spot in the centre of a clearing, where he kicked at a pile of fallen leaves. His foot made a hollow, wooden noise, and as he scraped back the detritus a wooden base became visible.

'There's the hole,' he told them. 'I'm surprised you didn't know about it, since it were the sheriff what ordered it, and Master Francis here's his bailiff.'

Edward's eyes narrowed as he stared at Gullen accusingly.

'You claim that you were told that this was intended as some sort of trapdoor for conducting future hangings, but when we hanged Amos Hutchins you said nothing about it, but simply conducted the process in the normal way. Then, when we called later to enquire about the nightly horrors that were being staged here, you made no mention of it either. You must have realised by then that this platform, and the hole that it conceals, was being used for something far more devious than hanging condemned men, but you *still* said nothing. Why am I finding it hard to believe in your innocence? You were far more involved in what went on here than you're prepared to admit, weren't you?'

'No — *honest!*' Gullen protested.

'How does this wooden platform get opened?' Francis asked.

'I've no idea — honest I don't!'

'I may be of assistance there,' Burridge chimed in. 'We need to look for some sort of winding mechanism that's probably hidden somewhere in the surrounding undergrowth. It won't be far away.'

'Where is it?' Edward demanded angrily as he grabbed the collar of Gullen's tunic, but the man continued to shake his head and claim ignorance of how the trapdoor was operated. Telling Giles to keep a firm grip on his 'prisoner', Edward followed Burridge's advice and the three of them began searching for something unusual in the undergrowth. It was Francis who found it several minutes later, as he gave a loud curse and fell into the leaf litter from the recent autumn fall. He got up, rubbing his bruised ankle, and stared down at what had caught his foot.

'There's some sort of pipe sticking out of the ground here!' he called to Edward and Burridge, who walked over to where he was standing. Burridge crouched down and felt it.

'It's almost certainly the base of a lever, connected to the platform underground. If you dig down for the few feet between this and the platform, you'll find either a rope or a series of levers, but it might be quicker to find the rest of the upper part of it. It'll be a metal bar, perhaps four or five feet long, that fits onto the base so that the entire device can be worked backwards and forwards.'

Edward turned to Gullen and demanded, 'Where is it?'

Gullen shook his head. 'I don't know, honest! All I did was help dig the hole.'

Edward nodded towards Giles. 'Take this man back inside his cottage, bind him at the wrists and ankles, then make a search for a metal bar, or something similar. Something that might be used as a lever.'

Giles walked back to the cottage with his sword drawn, pulling an ashen-faced Gullen by the sleeve of his tunic, and Edward, Francis and Burridge commenced a search of the remainder of the copse. After only a minute Burridge gave a shout of triumph and held up what looked like a piece of heavily scorched cloth.

'Look here! The remains of a squib! They were lucky that they did not set the entire wood on fire.'

'How do these things work?' Edward asked.

Burridge held the cloth up for them to view. 'You make a pouch out of cloth or thick vellum,' he explained, 'then you fill it with gunpowder and attach a slow fuse. You light the fuse and launch it into the air with some sort of catapult just as it starts to emit sparks. After a few seconds it will explode with a loud bang, and sparks will descend on those below. The effect is most effective at night, of course, and from what you tell me these were seen to rise out of the ground and fly through the air. They were almost certainly launched from the space beneath the trapdoor that we have already located, although they would have been a considerable danger to those launching them, since they do not always go off as planned.'

'That solves another mystery,' said Edward, then looked back with raised eyebrows to where Giles was returning, dragging Gullen with one hand and holding a metal cylinder in the other, approximately four feet in length.

'I found this under his bolster, sirs,' Giles told them, and Burridge took it eagerly from his hand and walked over to the metal stanchion that they'd discovered earlier. He placed the cylinder over the top of the stanchion and began working it backwards and forwards as if operating a water pump.

'Stand well back!' he instructed the rest of them as a grinding noise preceded the rapid disappearance of the wooden platform into the ground.

'This was the noise that preceded the appearance of the ghostly skull,' said Edward. 'At dead of night, if you could not see what was happening, you might easily mistake the sound for the opening of the gates of Hell.'

'Let's just hope there are no more demons in residence down there,' Francis joked feebly as he peered into the rapidly emerging hole in the ground. Giles had grown tired of hanging on to Gullen, and was in the process of tying him to a nearby tree.

The grinding noise eventually ceased, and the platform appeared to have travelled down for five or six feet. Edward lowered himself gingerly down into it, then gave an excited shout. 'There's a side chamber of some sort down here, and it seems to lead further down!'

Francis and Burridge jumped down onto the platform as Edward moved into the side chamber, guided by what appeared to be a glimmer of light from lower down. Eventually he found himself at ground level, in a small cave that was part of the network of caves at the base of the wooded cliff on which they'd been standing. As Francis and Burridge scrambled out after him, Francis allowed himself a wry chuckle.

'This explains how Agnes was able to make good her escape after her performance as a witch during the hanging. If she hid in that side passage, she wouldn't have been visible either from the wood at the top or at ground level among all these caves.'

'Then why did you not see the hole in the ground?' Edward asked. 'And how was it operated in broad daylight?'

'I take it that following her appearance, it was all chaos and consternation?' Burridge asked, and both men nodded. 'Then you have your answer,' he added. 'The hatch was already open when she made her appearance, presumably out of the ground?'

'No, seemingly out of nowhere,' Edward corrected him. 'She just seemed to come from somewhere in the crowd, and she leapt onto the cart that had brought the condemned man up here from the town gaol. He'd been hanged by then, so the cart was empty.'

'And everyone's eyes were on his final struggles?' Burridge asked.

Edward conceded the point, and Burridge smiled. 'The first rule of theatre — distract the audience with something else when you want to change the scene on stage. With us it was a dancer, or a man playing a sackbut. Even, perhaps, a couple of jugglers. So the trapdoor is already open, then during the general consternation after the woman's dire warning the hangman hurries to close it, using the method we have already discovered.'

'But surely I would have seen him?' Francis argued.

Burridge shook his head. 'You were intent on finding a fleeing woman, were you not? Your eyes would have been anticipating nothing else. An entire herd of cattle could have been up there without you noticing them.'

'Look what's here!' Edward suddenly shouted as he reached down into the sandy floor on which they were standing and came up with what looked like a human skull with red eyes. 'We've seen this before, haven't we, Francis? Except that when we saw it, there were flames coming from the eyes, and it was hanging in mid-air.'

'You have presumably been inside one of our former magnificent churches, or perhaps an abbey, before they were razed to the ground for the stone to be used in nearby houses?' Burridge asked.

'Of course,' Edward replied, 'but so what?'

'Then you would have seen the stained glass — saints and other biblical characters depicted in the windows. Much of it survived the masons' demolition hammers, and you'll find many an example in wealthy country houses, like those in which my company, the Lincoln Players, have often performed in. See where the eyeholes in the skull have been filled with red glass? Behind them would have been lit candles, giving the effect, on a dark night, of a flickering glow. If your audience has been pre-prepared to see the souls of the living dead, they will not suspect them to have been constructed from anything as mundane as candles and glass.'

'Very well,' Edward countered with mounting irritation, 'then explain to us how this skull was floating in mid-air.'

'It wasn't,' Burridge replied confidently. 'It would either have been suspended from the surrounding tree branches, and released on cue, or held up on a pole from underneath. I strongly suspect the latter, since the former would have required considerable expertise and commendable timing. So, let us keep looking.'

Francis kicked casually at what appeared to be a ridge of loose sandstone, but which proved to be a wooden pole with a platform attached. He called out and held it up for inspection by Burridge, who nodded sagely as he pointed out the holes in the platform that corresponded to holes in the skull.

'Clearly, the skull was mounted on the platform, then candles were lit behind the eye sockets. See here, where you can still discern some candle grease. The pole would then be raised above ground level, and perhaps waved from side to side. The pole is some six feet in height, and a woman, say five feet tall, would be barely a foot below ground level when standing on the lowered platform. All too easy to make the skull appear to be floating five feet above ground level.'

'There is one final matter,' Edward announced. 'The woman who was pretending to be speaking on behalf of Satan during these displays sounded as if she was calling to us from the depths of Hell, with a sepulchral voice. But the woman we have confined in a cell speaks like any other woman.'

'She spoke with what sounded like an echo?' Burridge asked, and Edward nodded. Burridge began searching through the various items lying scattered across the sandy floor, then gave a shout as he lifted up what looked like a milkmaid's metal jug. A few moments later he also pounced on a large cow horn. He lifted the horn to his mouth, inserted it into the top of the metal jug, then boomed out: 'Behold, the instruments of the Devil!'

Edward and Francis jumped at the sheer volume and dramatic effect, and Burridge offered an apologetic smile. 'Is there anything else I can reveal?'

'No,' Edward said grudgingly. 'I think that accounts for all that we were witness to. But we must collect all these items, ahead of revealing them to Master Parkin. I propose that we do not hazard a return through the secret passage, but walk round the long way, until we take the slope up to where Giles has Master Gullen safely attached to a tree.'

They puffed and grunted their way back up the slope and did their best to attach their discoveries to the saddlebags of their horses, before giving up the hopeless task with curses. It was Edward who suggested that Francis ride back into town and return with a cart. He then handed over a shilling from his tunic pocket.

'Acquire us a few mutton pies while you're about it, Francis,' he said.

'Why can't you go?' Francis complained.

'For one thing I'm no longer a bailiff, and never *was* a town bailiff.'

'But you're a senior constable of the Town Watch,' Francis reminded him. 'Why may I not command you to go back into the town to fetch the cart?'

'If you do so, you will need to hand me back that shilling,' said Edward, 'and believe me when I assure you that there will be no room on the cart for any mutton pies for you two. But perhaps more to the point, I need to ask a certain man currently tied to a tree to confirm our suspicions of what we have discovered this morning.'

18

'The master's in the main hall with his visitor,' Stokely's steward told Edward, Francis and Burridge as they called in at the sheriff's Stoney Street residence later that same day, after leaving Gullen to be processed down in the Guildhall cells. Stokely rose to greet them, and ordered that wine and wafers be served, ahead of a supper that he invited the three visitors to share. 'But lose no time in telling us how you fared at Gallows Hill, since Master Parkin here needs to send an urgent despatch down to Cecil in London.'

'We have much to impart,' Edward told them, clearly forgetting that Francis was now his official superior, and should have been the one presenting their findings. 'The man Gullen, our local hangman, was apparently so apprehensive of a meeting with the Tower torturers that he volunteered as much as he knew. We can now make public the fact that the apparent ghostly manifestations were no more than illusions created by those skilled in the theatrical arts, and we've brought back the evidence of that. There was a hole in the ground…'

'You brought back a hole in the ground?' Parkin asked jocularly, and everyone laughed.

'No,' Edward continued, 'but the hole in the ground concealed a hidden trapdoor in the copse across from the gallows themselves through which the illusions were produced.'

'And Gullen was the man who dug that hole?' Stokely asked.

'He was certainly the one who was present when it was dug, with his connivance. It seems that the authorisation for that came from Sheriff Kniveton.'

'We suspected as much,' Parkin replied with a sage nod. 'But what of the other theatrical devices?'

'Very basic, but very effective,' Burridge told them.

Edward hastened to introduce Sheriff Stokely to Henry Burridge.

'He's the leader of a troupe of wandering players, and is very experienced in the methods employed to create theatrical illusions. It was he who advised us, when we found the first indication of how the platform was raised and lowered, that there must be a lever by which it was operated. Gullen, who had previously feigned ignorance of anything beyond the digging of the hole, was found to have possession of a lever that, when operated, brought a platform up and down through the hole, which was some five feet in depth, and connected with a chamber that led down into the old caves inhabited by the lowest in our community. It was at this point that Gullen was threatened with a journey to the Tower, that I strongly recommend he not be required to undertake.'

'How can you explain away the rest?' Stokely asked eagerly. 'The townsfolk need to be reassured that all is well, and that they are not about to be consumed by devils.'

'Again, we are indebted to Master Burridge,' Edward said. 'The sound of the portals of Hell being opened was simply the grinding of the mechanism that opened the platform below ground, the flaming skull was nothing more fiendish than stained glass and candles held up on a pole, and the ghostly voice was that of Agnes Merryweather, who recently escaped being condemned as a witch, but should be put on trial without delay for her connivances.'

'What could this man Gullen tell you, if anything, about who might have been behind all this, other than Kniveton?' Parkin asked.

'While Master Burridge here was being deservedly released from any charges he might have faced regarding the recent antics of some of his troupe in Newark, Francis and I took the opportunity to remind Master Gullen of the various devices employed in the Tower. It was then that he seemed to recall the attendance at Gallows Hill of a man called Henstridge, who was the one who instructed Gullen and Mistress Merryweather regarding the production of the theatrical effects. Seemingly he was well versed in them, although even under threat of being stretched on the rack Gullen was unable to advise us regarding who had sent him.'

'I may be able to assist in that matter also,' Burridge chimed in. 'Did this man Henstridge by any chance have the first name Barclay, did Gullen say?'

'No,' Francis replied. 'But he *did* give us a description of the man's appearance. In his own words, he was "Large, bald-headed and dissolute-looking, like a monk thrown out of holy orders for drinking too much wine." Does that help?'

'It most certainly does,' Burridge beamed back in confirmation, 'since it's a perfect description of a man called Barclay Henstridge, who was until recently a leading performer in my troupe. He is a consummate actor, but too fond of the fruits of the vine, and we parted company acrimoniously following a series of performances we gave at a noble house some miles north of here. We were on our way back to Lincoln from there, performing in Newark, when I was taken up by the constables. Barclay claimed to have been offered work on the estate of the man we had been performing for, and to be perfectly candid with you I heaved a sigh of relief to be rid of him.'

Kniveton and Parkin exchanged excited glances, and Parkin asked, 'Do you recall the name of this noble estate, where Henstridge was offered employment?'

'Of course,' Burridge replied. 'One does not forget an estate so grand, or a patron so generous in his rewards for our somewhat mediocre representations of the lives of the saints. His name was Byron, and his estate was called Newstead. Does that assist?'

'Yes!' Edward yelled before he had time to suppress his delight. 'We have him, and God be praised that he dismissed me from his service before I could be implicated in his devious schemes. I dearly hope that I shall be the one sent to arrest him!'

'No-one will be sent to arrest him until we have clearance from Cecil,' Parkin announced sombrely. 'There is much more we must learn regarding the background activities of your former employer before we may lay hands on him.'

'Who is he, anyway?' Burridge asked, nonplussed at the reaction that his explanation had provoked. 'I know that he is the Sheriff of the County, and that he has influential friends at court. I also know that he is well connected to royalty, or so he boasted.'

'Tell us more, please!' Parkin urged him.

Burridge screwed up his face as he did his best to recall the precise details. 'I can only vaguely recollect an evening during which we were staging the life and death of Saint Stephen, the first martyr. Our patron had invited several guests from another estate that I recall was somewhere further north. Among them a rather frosty old lady, along with her granddaughter, a somewhat pallid and withdrawn creature, and I was greatly surprised when our host introduced her as the next Queen of England, since I know that our current queen has no heirs.'

'It gets better!' Parkin cried, before explaining his reaction to Burridge and the others. 'The young lady in question was almost certainly Arbella Stuart, and we now have proof of her connection with Byron. I must lose no time in riding to Nottingham Castle to dispatch a fast messenger down to London, for advice from Cecil on how to proceed with this invaluable information.'

'Can we not simply arrest Byron first?' Francis asked.

Parkin shook his head. 'For what, precisely? Hosting a religious pageant?'

'But he was openly consorting with a contender for the English crown!' Francis persisted, to a withering look from Parkin.

'If that be an act worthy of arrest, then Cecil himself could be taken up, on charges based on his frequent meetings with James of Scotland. The sad truth is that *no-one* may be spoken of as Elizabeth's successor in her lifetime, unless she nominates her own heir.'

Edward had been thinking hard. 'Is Byron known to be close with the Earl of Essex? Is that why Cecil is so eager to be advised of any plot to advance the cause of Arbella Stuart?'

Parkin stared at him. 'You would seem to be wasted here in Nottingham, Master Mountsorrel. It is no secret that on his frequent visits to London Byron is an honoured guest at Leicester House, Essex's residence in The Strand. For that reason, like every other good friend of Robert Devereux, Cecil keeps a close watch on Byron's activities and other connections. If we can demonstrate a connection between Byron and the family resident at Hardwick Hall, then Cecil will be able to employ it in his constant battles with Essex for the queen's ear, particularly on the matter of the succession.'

'I don't pretend to follow the subtleties of matters at court,' Edward said, 'but what do you wish us to do next?'

Parkin thought briefly before replying. 'Clearly, the connection between Kniveton and Byron is no secret, but the next step must be to acquire evidence of Byron's involvement in the artifices at Gallows Hill. From what Master Burridge has been able to tell us, it would seem that the man who assisted in the staging of those events was introduced by Kniveton himself, who must, one assumes, have been instructed to employ him by Byron. I suggest that our next step should be to subject Sheriff Kniveton to questioning designed to elicit the truth of that supposition.'

'I shall take great pleasure in being a party to that,' said Francis, before Stokely sounded a word of caution.

'When I last called upon him — only yesterday — he claimed to be too indisposed to be able to receive visitors, although he was clearly spying on my attendance from a window.'

'Indisposed?' Parkin said, bristling. 'He will be even more indisposed when we break down his door and shake him by the throat to see what answers fall from his mouth. You forget that I act with the authority of the Secretary of State. Come, let us get this over without delay, in order that we may enjoy our supper on our return.'

Kniveton's steward looked nervously at the four well-dressed men demanding to speak with his employer, and the two serious-looking men at arms who loomed ominously behind them. He'd only opened the door wide enough to see who was calling at such a late hour of the working day. 'My master left earlier today, and took clothing with him for a few days' visit to his friend the county sheriff.'

'We may assume that he's recovered from the malady that rendered him unfit even to receive visitors yesterday?' Stokely asked sarcastically, but the steward opted for silence.

'Come, gentlemen,' Parkin responded, 'we are clearly wasting our time here, and supper awaits us elsewhere.'

Back at Stokely's house, around the supper table, it was Edward who voiced what he and Francis were both thinking.

'A visit to Newstead would seem to be in order.'

'Indeed,' Parkin confirmed, 'but not a formal one with men at arms. Not yet, anyway.'

'What would you suggest?' Edward asked.

'Something more subtle is required, but its precise nature does not yet suggest itself to me. We need to be certain that Kniveton may be found at Newstead, along with this man Henstridge, before we even begin to question Byron regarding his associations and loyalties. But the enquiries in order to establish those facts must be conducted clandestinely, and you are known to Byron by sight, while Barton will be well known to Kniveton.'

'Even *better* known, when we have done with him,' Francis said, then a thought struck him. 'But Edward and I are well acquainted with someone who could venture innocently onto the Newstead estate, and investigate who might be found there.'

Edward raised an enquiring eyebrow.

'A certain lady who might have occasion to call there in an effort to sell her recent apple crop?'

'You mean Kitty?'

'Who else? She will have a passable excuse for visiting the house, and will not be recognised. Added to which, she is very

184

resourceful and gifted with a ready wit. All we need to do is supply her with a description of the man Henstridge; she will of course recognise Byron from when she attended your trial.'

'Then there is also the risk that Byron will recognise her,' Edward objected.

'Do you have a better idea?'

'No, to be perfectly candid. But you will be asking her to hazard her own safety.'

'She will no doubt be more than happy to oblige. She swore vengeance against Byron for what he put Rose through.'

'I do not know these ladies of whom you speak,' said Parkin, 'but Francis's suggestion has a lot to recommend it. Can you be certain that this lady, Kitty, can be persuaded?'

'If anyone is capable of persuading her, it is Francis,' Edward assured him, not entirely sure that he was comfortable with what was being suggested.

'We were clearly correct in not saving you any supper,' Elizabeth said coldly when Edward came home for long enough to pack a bag and advise her that early the following morning he and Francis were riding north in the service of Secretary of State Robert Cecil. 'And has Master Cecil also guaranteed that your wife and children will still be here when you return?'

Edward sighed. 'It is perhaps as well that I am no longer a bailiff, since once this latest business is concluded I may spend more time at home, where, it would seem, my presence is required on a more regular basis.'

'And what will you do to see us fed?' Elizabeth demanded. 'You'll find your best tunic hanging in the rear garden, where Meg hung it to dry, if that's what you're searching for under the bolster.'

'No, I was looking for my heavy staff — the one issued to me as a senior constable in Francis's service.'

'I put that under your spare linen at the top of the closet, in case the children found it and began to wreck the house with it. Why do you need it, anyway, and where exactly are you off to?'

'Daybrook, to visit Rose and Kitty. As you may recall, Kitty is the one who has ambitions to become Mistress Barton.'

'And you need the protection of your constable's staff against Francis's intended?' she asked sarcastically.

'No, but Francis might, if he keeps her waiting much longer for a marriage proposal. Then, in further answer to your question, we are headed to Newstead.'

'You intend to assault the Sheriff of Nottinghamshire for dismissing you?'

'No, something much more satisfying. We shall be exposing him as the man behind all those dreadful manifestations at Gallows Hill — you remember, the ones you were so anxious for me to put to an end?'

'As I recall,' Elizabeth replied, as she began to disrobe, 'I urged you to stay well away from them, in the same way that I make frequent requests for you to spend more time at home.'

'Because you wish to dissuade me from what I must do?'

'No, because I love you, although God alone knows that there are times when I wonder why, and whether or not you deserve it. So join me beneath the covers and remind me why I persevere with you, while I give you something that will ensure you don't forget where you live when you're done with traipsing the countryside in pursuit of what you seem to regard as matters of higher priority.'

'I really don't deserve you,' Edward murmured as he slid in beside her and held her to him.

'No, you don't,' she replied, as tears appeared in her eyes, 'but you might wish to work towards doing so. I don't want this to be the last time we do this.'

Kitty ran eagerly from the cottage as the two men approached, and was waiting to embrace Francis warmly as he slid down from the saddle. 'I was hoping you'd be back soon,' she said, 'because we have plans to make, if you're to keep your promise.'

'There's something else we need before we get down to that,' Francis told her, and she nodded.

'Dinner will be ready as soon as Rose finishes setting the board.'

'Something other than that,' Edward added. 'We wish you to assist us to bring down Sheriff Byron.'

'It's long past the time that somebody did,' Rose agreed from the open doorway, 'but you're asking the wrong person. *I'm* the one with a score to settle.'

'And you're the one he'd remember from your trial,' Edward reminded her.

'For which I'll always be in your debt,' Rose said, smiling at him. 'And before you insist that it was in repayment of a service that I once performed for you, I may tell you that you don't need to advise me that your son has made a full recovery from his early melancholy, as I already know.'

'Unless you can also, with your second sight, advise us of what is currently occurring on the Newstead estate, we need to enlist Kitty's services,' Edward replied as the four of them made their way into the cottage, where Rose poured them each a mug of elderberry wine and began laying out the utensils for dinner.

'What do you require of me?' Kitty asked as she sat next to Francis, holding his hand. 'And what has it to do with Sheriff Byron?'

Edward explained the need to make enquiry into the possible presence, inside the converted abbey, of the Sheriff of Nottingham, William Kniveton, and a man called Barclay Henstridge, whose physical description he gave her. 'I cannot fully disclose why we need to know these things, but we cannot approach the house ourselves, since we would be too easily recognised. You, on the other hand, could approach the kitchen door on the pretence of selling apples, and might then find some ploy to gain admission to the rest of the house. Once you have the information we require, you could of course make a hasty departure.'

Kitty needed little persuasion, particularly when reminded by Rose that not only did they still need to repay Byron for accusing her of witchcraft, but they could take the opportunity to get their revenge on Kniveton for releasing Agnes Merryweather without charging her with any offence.

After dinner they loaded a cart with the remaining barrels from the annual crop, and with cheery waves of farewell to Rose they made their way out into the mid-afternoon sun, reaching the boundary of the Newstead estate just as the sun was dipping low on the western horizon. Francis kissed Kitty farewell and wished her good fortune as Edward stood politely looking the other way. A few minutes later, Kitty was talking to the cook regarding the prospect of unloading the remainder of her season's crop of apples at a bargain price.

'I'm not sure as we need as many as that,' the cook told her with a frown. 'The master's not one for fruit, as a rule, and I doesn't do a lot of baking, so four barrels would be too much, even at the fair price you're asking. But he's got guests staying at the moment, so perhaps… Look, stay here a minute and I'll go and ask if they'd like apple pastries for their dinner tomorrow.'

'Who are the guests?' Kitty asked in what she hoped was a tone of only casual interest.

The cook shrugged. 'One of them's the town sheriff up on business, and there's one from Hardwick, in Derbyshire. Quite an old lady, but ready-witted enough. And she's got a young lassie with her.'

'Actually,' Kitty added, before the cook could depart on her self-appointed enquiry, 'there was a lovely man I met in Papplewick a few days ago. He looked like a priest or a friar, and he said that he had business here in Newstead. A man called Barclay, from memory. Is he a guest here as well?'

In the corner of the kitchen was the open door to the scullery, through which an enquiring face peered cautiously, before its owner made her way stealthily out through the door into the stable yard to summon two men at arms. The cook was just returning to advise Kitty that she'd been authorised to buy only one of her barrels when the main kitchen door flew open, and two heavily armed men burst in, accompanied by Agnes Merryweather, who yelled an instruction.

'That's her — grab hold of her, and take her before the master. She might well be selling apples, but to my mind she's too interested in who might be hiding away here. Her sister's a witch, and likely she's no different, so the master may decide to have her taken out and burned.'

19

Kitty tried to ignore the curious rat staring at her from the far corner of the narrow room in which she'd been confined, and concentrated instead on silently cursing her old enemy Agnes Merryweather, who appeared to have won the latest round of their almost lifelong rivalry. Agnes had clearly not only escaped any punishment for her part in the false accusations of witchcraft against Rose, but appeared to have been afforded employment in the grand house that had been built on the ruins of the former Newstead Abbey.

It was not difficult to imagine how Agnes had wormed her way into service with Sheriff Byron, who was so obsessed with witchcraft that he was prepared to accuse innocent women of consorting with the Devil on the flimsiest of evidence, and had been easily seduced into pointing an accusing finger at Rose.

Poor, dear Rose, her older sister, her constant companion and guide through the early years of their lives, and the woman with the truest heart that Kitty had ever known. Perhaps, before she was dragged out, maybe to be put to death as a suspected witch herself, Kitty would close her eyes, concentrate on Rose, and try to absorb some of the love that always flowed so generously from her heart. There was virtually no light from the narrow pane of glass set high in the wall, so perhaps she might gain a little sleep in the process, to fortify herself against what might lie ahead.

Outside it was rapidly growing dark, and Edward and Francis were becoming increasingly worried. It had now been a few hours since Kitty had left her horse and cart by the kitchen door and disappeared inside the stately house. They were still where she'd left them, but there had been no further sign of her. Even if she'd been successful in obtaining the information she'd been sent inside to acquire, it shouldn't have taken this long, whereas if she'd been discovered, or simply just suspected, and then apprehended, it might explain why she'd failed to reappear at the kitchen door.

The two men were watching the side door to the house, behind which the kitchen presumably lay. Francis in particular was seriously contemplating rushing into the house with a drawn sword, and demanding to know what had happened to Kitty, even if it meant revealing their attempt to obtain information regarding Byron's involvement in recent events. Only Edward's constant reminders that their duty to Parkin, Cecil and the queen required that they reveal nothing about what they suspected, had so far prevented Francis remounting his horse and executing what would amount to a one-man assault on Newstead Hall, which was no doubt well supplied with armed retainers.

'It's all very well for you,' Francis accused Edward bitterly, 'since it was *your* idea, *your* ambition to get your own back on Byron, and *your* choice of who to send in there on a perilous mission.'

Edward looked him firmly in the eye. 'It was *your* idea to employ Kitty as our potential source of information, and we do not yet know what has transpired. For all we know, she's being fed by the cook, and is getting all the intelligence we require from her. You know how garrulous cooks are.'

Francis huffed. 'You seem to be overlooking the fact that she's the woman I love — the woman I've chosen to spend the rest of my days with.'

'Purely as a matter of interest, have you told her that?'

'What do you mean?'

'Have you told Kitty that you want to spend the rest of your life with her? The last conversation I heard between the two of you on that subject was before dinner yesterday, when you put the issue of possible marriage to one side in favour of what you deemed to be more important. Don't make the same mistake that I have, Francis, and let your duties get in the way of a happy home life. I secretly rejoice in the loss of my office, because it now leaves me free to pursue other means of earning a livelihood, although I know not what. Whatever I do, I intend to devote more time to my family.'

It fell silent as both men looked gloomily to the west, where the sun had disappeared behind a range of hills. They drew their cloaks around themselves and settled onto the ground in front of the low hedge that marked the estate boundary.

'Will you and Elizabeth be our witnesses?' Francis suddenly asked.

'Witnesses to what, precisely?' Edward asked, his grin hidden by the darkness that enveloped them. He was determined to milk the moment for all it was worth.

'My marriage to Kitty — assuming that she's still alive in there. The law requires two witnesses, as I understand it, and there's the matter of a priest. Should we enquire at St Nicholas's, which is our nearest parish church, or do you think that Kitty would prefer the parish church in Daybrook?'

'I have no idea,' Edward replied. 'Perhaps you should have enquired before allowing her to go inside Newstead Hall.'

'I swear to God, Edward,' Francis responded angrily, 'that if you weren't my best friend, I'd run you through for reminding me of that.'

'Save your blade for Byron's attendants,' Edward replied, 'and in the meantime try to sleep, for you will need all your wits about you when the sun rises on the morrow.'

It was well into the so-called 'dead hour' of the early morning before Francis, who had been barely dozing, was awoken by the faint sound of clothing brushing against foliage. He leapt to his feet, drew his sword and yelled a challenge into the darkness that woke Edward from an uneasy slumber.

'Is that any way to welcome family who come bearing victuals?' asked an amused voice as Rose appeared from the shadows, carrying a basket.

'How did *you* get here?' Edward asked, amazed by her sudden arrival.

Rose lowered herself to the ground and opened the basket to unleash the alluring aromas of fresh bread, cheese and dried fish.

'I know that Kitty's in danger. She's a prisoner in a room somewhere inside yon house. She's still alive, but I sense that will not be for long, unless we do something.'

'God be praised!' Francis muttered. 'But how did you know?'

'The second sight, which I have possessed all my life,' Rose replied. 'Kitty and I have been close to each other's hearts since she was born, and the gift is stronger if there are blood ties, or strong love between two people. Kitty and I have both in abundance, and she was obviously thinking of me while she lay in darkness and fear.'

'So you flew here on your broomstick?' Francis asked cheekily.

'Don't make me regret bringing you this food and wine, you impertinent oaf! As for how I got here, you obviously failed to hear the wheels of the wagon that Samuel Morton used to bring me here, under threat that if he did not there would be no more unctions for his facial warts. He's taken himself back to Daybrook with enough of my remedy to see him into next summer.'

'Now that you're here, what do you propose?' Edward asked as he pulled the stopper from the wine gourd and allowed the red nectar to flow into his mouth.

'That's surely for you to decide,' Rose replied, 'but go easy with that strawberry wine, if you want to have your wits about you come daybreak. Now let's feed our stomachs, then get some sleep, since I suspect that we're all going to be in much need of it if we are to rescue Kitty from the mess you've got her into.'

Edward awoke to the sound of hammering. He yawned, stretched, then looked back towards Newstead Hall for the source of the noise. He froze in horror.

On the well-tended lawn in front of the house, retainers under the supervision of a man who, even from that distance, closely resembled the description of Barclay Henstridge, were hammering a cross-like structure onto the top of two upright wooden poles that had been dug into the ground. Others were arranging a row of chairs under the front windows of the main building. Clearly they were preparing for a very public hanging. Edward had a grim idea of who was intended to be the main player in the entertainment, and he hastily woke Francis.

'On your feet, if you want to preserve your marriage prospects,' he instructed him, and the sound of his voice woke Rose.

She turned to follow Edward's gaze. 'Is that intended for Kitty, do you think?' she asked hoarsely.

Edward nodded. 'We must assume so, but let us hope that they intend to breakfast first, since that will afford us longer to plan our strategy.'

'*Strategy*?' Rose demanded angrily. 'Are you two officers of the law or not? An innocent woman is about to be strung up without trial, and you talk about *strategy*?'

'There are several reasons why we cannot just storm in and demand Kitty's release,' Edward attempted to explain. 'The first is that we would almost certainly be outnumbered. The second is that we are under orders from a man close to the throne to merely discover what we can regarding who is currently residing within the house, and their relationships with each other.'

'I'll give you two reasons of my own,' Rose replied sharply. 'The first is that Kitty is my dearly loved sister, and the intended of your colleague here. The second is that I have means of my own with which to get what I want.'

'Some sort of new magic?' Edward asked sceptically.

'No — magic of the *old* description,' Rose snarled. 'Just accompany me down there, and prepare to untie Kitty and bring her here to safety, whatever they may threaten to do to me.'

'Did I hear you correctly?' asked Francis. 'You intend to just walk down there and turn them all into toads?'

'No, you clod — I'm intending to turn you into a bridegroom,' Rose retorted. 'Now, get behind me, both of you!'

They were a strange sight as they strode in a determined group down the drive to the front of the house, coming to a halt a few feet from where the gallows had just been completed. Out of the house walked Byron, accompanied by Kniveton and an elderly lady whose arm was being gripped firmly by a pale-looking girl who could have passed for a personal maid, but who was almost certainly Arbella Stuart. The recently emerged party seemed too intent on deciding who should occupy which seat to even notice that they had new arrivals, until Rose took a deep breath and bellowed, 'A murrain on this house!'

Byron looked up sharply from where he had been shepherding the old lady into the most comfortable seat. 'You!' he yelled back. 'You should have hanged as a witch!'

'Indeed I should, but like all wise women I was well protected by those who enjoy being favoured by those of us with knowledge of the old ways — the *dark* ways!'

'Who is this woman, John?' the old lady asked nervously.

'An old hag who was recently tried before me for witchcraft,' Byron replied. 'She escaped justice by sleight of hand employed by the man on her right, who is my former bailiff, and who has clearly fallen under her wicked spell. But although she didn't hang, there is hope yet for her sister. Bring out the prisoner!' he shouted to a heavily armed retainer, who disappeared inside, emerging moments later prodding Kitty forward on the end of a sword.

She was tied at her wrists and ankles, forcing her to walk with an awkward shuffle, and she had been stripped of all her clothing except her undershift, a plain off-white garment that extended to her knees. She squinted into the bright morning light, then called out in Francis's direction, 'The man Henstridge is here — he's the one with the rope in his hands.'

'The rope by which you will be hanged until the sin has been choked from your soul,' Byron spat. 'We had insufficient time in which to construct a funeral pyre, but you will experience the fires of Hell soon enough!'

'Is she adjudged a witch?' the old lady asked.

Byron shrugged. 'We have no time for all that "ordeal" nonsense that failed to unmask her wicked sister, but there are other reasons why she must die. For one thing, she clearly knows too much about our plans for the future.'

'So the woman *is* a witch?' the old lady asked as she rose from her chair and held out her hand for her young companion. 'Come, Arbella, and let us summon the coachman to take us back to Hardwick. This place is not safe for us!'

'Please remain, Countess!' Byron called after her pleadingly. 'She was adjudged not to be a witch, and there is nothing to fear from her.'

'Just because I was cleared of witchcraft does not mean that I am *not* a daughter of Satan!' Rose called out in a harsh voice. 'One who can ride under the moon on the feasts of All Hallows, Beltane and Walpurgis, and assume the likeness of the familiar that feeds on my third nipple, hidden to all but the initiates of my ancient order. Untie my sister, or I will smite you with the Black Death, drop your cattle where they stand at pasture, and infest your servants with worms that will eat away their innards. Unhand her, I say!'

The countess and her young granddaughter had disappeared around the side of the house, and the retainers stood rooted in fear as the sound of distant hooves could be heard approaching down the main drive. Edward looked behind him and gave a loud cheer as he spotted the gold lions passant on the tunics of a dozen men at arms who were clattering down the slope, accompanying a somewhat red-faced Matthew Parkin who called for everyone to remain where they were.

He dismounted and walked across to Edward after ordering his men to take command of the situation, despatching four of them to stop and surround the coach that had just emerged from the stable yard to the side.

'I assume that those were your horses tied to those trees at the entrance? If so, I shall send men to bring them down here,' said Parkin. 'It would seem that we came just in the nick of time.'

'Indeed you did, but how did you know?' asked Edward.

'Clearly I did not, but I determined that my broadly worded mission from Cecil entitled me to make immediate use of whatever further information you might have unearthed. I was uneasy that I might have exposed you all to further danger, so I chose to arrive accompanied by men from the royal garrison at Nottingham. I was correct, apparently, since we seem to have interrupted a hanging that I assume was not lawfully condoned?'

'Indeed it was not,' Edward confirmed. 'The intended victim was a lady called Catherine Fellows — Kitty — shortly to become Mistress Barton, and she can confirm the presence here at Newstead of the man Henstridge, who was under instruction from Byron to raise panic among the people of Nottingham. In the carriage that you instructed your men to seize you will, I suspect, find the lady known as Arbella Stuart and her grandmother.'

'Excellent!' Parkin said with a smile. 'Now you must leave me to conduct my mission as I deem appropriate, and I will meet with you again, two days hence, at the house of Sheriff Stokely — let us say for dinner.'

'I shall be delighted to learn of the outcome of your mission,' Edward said as he held out his hand to shake Parkin's. 'Now I intend to take my leave of you, once my friend and companion has freed his bride-to-be.'

While they had been talking, Francis had raced over and embraced Kitty, who kissed him passionately. 'If you untie my hands, I will hug you,' she promised, as tears began to roll down her cheeks.

'That will depend upon whether or not you agree to marry me within the month,' Francis replied as he fought back tears of his own.

20

There were smiles all round as Edward and Francis were welcomed to the dinner table inside Stokely's house in Stoney Street. Parkin afforded them a warm welcome, and Stokely instructed that the board be laid for the meal, but both their faces suggested that the news they had to impart might not be what their two guests had been expecting to hear. Parkin cleared his throat to speak.

'Congratulations once again, gentlemen. I am delighted to be able to report that I have been able to put in place the broad instructions I brought north from Secretary Cecil, and to send him a despatch confirming your success in unmasking what appears to have been another chapter in an ongoing conspiracy. But thanks to you the path of James of Scotland to the throne of England has been cleared of immediate obstacles — not that he will be required to take the road south in the immediate future, of course. That is the good news.'

'And the not so good?' Edward asked.

'The not so good, as you call it, is that I was, and still am, under orders from Cecil as to how to move matters on, and the actions I was obliged to take were as subtle and — well, underhand might best describe it — as you might expect from that wily son of an even more wily father. Bear in mind that the Cecils, between them, have been the power behind Elizabeth's throne for her entire reign, and that England is much stronger for their services.'

'How bad *is* the news?' Edward asked gloomily as the first course was brought in by two servants, who bowed out as silently as they had entered.

Parkin frowned. 'We may begin with the Countess of Salisbury and her granddaughter.'

'She was the old lady preparing to watch Mistress Fellows hang?' Francis asked. 'I recall Byron calling her "Countess".'

Parkin nodded. 'She is known more commonly as Bess of Hardwick. The young lady with her was Arbella Stuart, around whom the plot was being constructed, possibly without her active connivance, or even perhaps her knowledge.'

'I've advised Francis of the background,' Edward confirmed, eager to hear the bad news. 'I take it that they have not been apprehended and charged with anything?'

'Indeed not,' Parkin confirmed, 'although they *are* headed for a period of what might best be described as close confinement in London.'

'But not in the Tower?' Edward persevered.

'Indeed not. To be precise, they have both been summoned to Westminster — by Cecil, not by Her Majesty. But it is Cecil's intention to suggest to Elizabeth that the countess, as befits her dowager status, be made a senior lady at court, so that he can keep a closer eye on her. As for the granddaughter Arbella, a suitable match would seem to be in order. She is over twenty-one years of age, and is said by those who report to Cecil from within the household at Hardwick Hall to be eager to marry, if only to get away from her grandmother, whose rule over her has become somewhat oppressive of late. The match that Cecil has in mind will be a pliant and harmless Protestant fop from a distant county, and as far distant as possible from any possibility of Catholic intrigue. Once she is safely married off, Essex will hopefully abandon any ambition to steal her heart.'

'So, far from being justly punished for their plots against England's true interests, as perceived by Cecil, the countess and her nestling are to be favoured with positions at court?' Edward replied angrily.

'You will have to believe me when I say that life at court under the scrutiny of Robert Cecil could hardly be described as a reward for services rendered.'

'What of Essex himself?' Francis asked.

Parkin sighed. 'Even more of Cecil's subtlety, I'm afraid, but hear me out before you howl in protest. Robert Devereux has for some time been seeking the honour of leading Elizabeth's troops in Ireland, where in recent years there has been much unrest. Cecil has been opposing such a proposal, but has now decided to withdraw his opposition, in the hope that it will prove fatal to his old rival at court. His thinking is that either Essex will be killed by the enemy, or — given that he is regarded by those who know these things to be a most incompetent military commander — he might be assassinated by his own men. Alternatively, perhaps he will make such a botch of proceedings that he will fall out of favour with Her Majesty.'

'One would clearly not wish to fall foul of Cecil,' Edward said with a chuckle. 'But what of Sheriffs Byron and Kniveton? Surely they cannot have escaped immediate retribution for what they were involved in?'

Parkin took a deep breath. 'They have both been effectively stripped of their power. In the case of Kniveton, it's well known that he is interested only in the status that the office carries, and not the duties that it entails. Sheriff Stokely can more than carry out those duties, given a competent and loyal bailiff such as Barton here.'

Francis opened his mouth to speak, but Parkin raised a hand to silence him.

'As for Byron, he is a different consideration. However, he has been advised that his involvement in recent irregular events, and in particular his disgraceful promotion of panic in the community and false allegations of witchcraft, will only be overlooked if he agrees to stand down, pleading illness, and allowing a search to commence for his successor. He was led to believe that this would take some time, although I have already sounded out John Thorold, and he is primed to assume the duties of County Sheriff a month earlier than would normally have been the case, that is in February of next year.'

'And if Sheriff Byron is to do nothing until then, and given that he currently has no bailiff, what is to happen to law and order in the county?' Edward demanded in disbelief.

Parkin and Stokely exchanged embarrassed looks before Francis coughed nervously and supplied the answer.

'*I* am to happen to law and order in the county, Edward,' he mumbled, then looked down awkwardly at the fish on his trencher.

'The truth is,' said Parkin, 'I called on Francis late yesterday and asked if he would accept the office of county bailiff. You must realise that you are even less acceptable to Byron now than you were before, and he blankly refused to even consider reinstating you. Such is the importance of securing his compliance with our proposals for the termination of his office at an early date that we had to make that concession. I was also advised by Sheriff Stokely here that Francis had raised with him, on an earlier occasion, the prospect of his resignation from town duties in order to assist his wife-to-be in the management of her fruit business. But there is more good news.'

'Good news for the county, certainly,' Edward admitted through gritted teeth, 'but hardly for the town. Who is to be *my* new supervisor?'

'Me,' Stokely replied quietly, 'if you will accept the office of town bailiff, which of course becomes vacant when Francis takes up his new position in the county.'

Edward turned to Francis with a broad grin. 'We appear to be exchanging offices.'

'Indeed,' said Francis, smiling back. 'And I shall expect to find that brandy bottle still secreted away in the cupboard of my new office. *And* for it to remain half full.'

The wedding service over, everyone was getting steadily drunk inside Francis's house on Whitefriars Lane. Even the Reverend Lambe, Rector of St Nicholas's Church, where Kitty Fellows had become Mistress Catherine Barton. The wine was flowing freely, and all attempt at food service had been abandoned when Francis's houseboy Ralph had led Meg by the hand into his living quarters above the kitchen, where they had been clandestinely meeting for months, unknown to both families.

A red-faced Rose was swaying genteelly backwards and forwards, threatening to turn Francis into a toad if he in any way abused her sister now that they were married, while Elizabeth was standing to one side with Margaret held by one hand and Robert by the other, grinning from ear to ear as she experienced the benefits of a third mug of Rose's elderberry wine.

'I'm sure I'll be *very* well looked after,' Kitty asserted after the hiccups abated, adding with a sly glance at Francis, 'After all, he'll be too tired after being up all night.'

'I can't promise to maintain that service forever,' Francis leered back, to a disapproving tut from Elizabeth, a knowing grin from Rose, and a peal of laughter from Kitty.

'That's not what I meant,' said Kitty. 'I meant the lack of sleep that comes from having a tiny baby bawling for food.'

Francis paused to absorb her words. 'You mean — I mean — that is, you're…'

'Indeed. I shall soon be letting out my bodice, so you didn't marry me a day too soon.'

Edward let out a bark of mocking laughter. 'Caught in a web of your own weaving!' he exclaimed. 'The bird has found its roost! *Now* you'll need to keep closer to your own hearth!'

'Like *you* have?' Elizabeth asked with heavy irony as she gave Kitty a sympathetic smile. 'Don't expect him to be home for meals — only for night-time activities.'

'And you never complained of those,' Edward reminded her. 'Thanks to my occasional appearances we now have two beautiful children.'

Rose looked enquiringly across at Elizabeth.

'Is now a good time to tell him? Or do you perhaps not yet know yourself?'

'Know what?' Elizabeth asked as her face reddened.

Rose shook her head with a chuckle. 'Lord love us, some people know nothing about the workings of their own bodies. Your family of four will shortly become five. The way you are standing reveals it all to a woman who is wise regarding the workings of nature.'

'How can you be sure?' Edward asked.

'Didn't they tell you?' Rose asked with amusement. 'I'm reckoned to be a witch.'

A NOTE TO THE READER

Dear Reader,

Thank you for investing your valuable reading time in this latest novel in the Bailiff Mountsorrel Tudor Mystery series, and I hope that it lived up to your expectations. As with the previous novels in the series, it gave me particular pleasure to be able to research the Elizabethan history of the town in which I lived for the first twenty-one years of my life.

Gallows Hill, which features so prominently in the plotline, was indeed the place appointed for public hangings in Nottingham during the Tudor period, and it remained so until the final hanging there in 1827. These days the site is better known as Church Cemetery, or Rock Cemetery, and it still sits on the same junction of Mansfield Road and what is now Forest Road. It is a tribute to the Victorian obsession with grave ornaments, and as a schoolboy I spent many happy hours wandering among the ornate tombstones of long-dead civic worthies, shivering as I passed the spot where the gallows once stood. These days, however, the only regularly reported ghost is that of a quaint little old lady dressed in Victorian attire who vanishes from sight if challenged.

If you haven't read the previous novels in this series, then I should explain why there were two sheriffs, and two bailiffs, for two separate jurisdictions whose functions sometimes overlapped. Prior to 1449, and contrary to the Robin Hood myth, there was no Sheriff of Nottingham as such, but a High Sheriff of Nottinghamshire whose remit covered the town as well as the surrounding county. Then in that year Nottingham was granted a civic charter that made it self-governing, and with it came a new guardian of law and order in the town.

From the outset the duties were seemingly so onerous that the post of Sheriff of Nottingham was held jointly by two men, who without exception were also wealthy local merchants, and usually associated in some way with the Corporation that governed the town's business affairs. According to my research, those in office in 1596 were indeed William Kniveton and George Stokely, although very little else is known about them. I employed what might politely be described as artistic licence in describing their characters, and my apologies to any living descendants of the former, who probably wasn't as conniving and bombastic as I depicted him.

There was, however, only one sheriff for the county, and in 1596 it was Sir John Byron of Newstead, in respect of whom I repeat my plea of artistic licence and apology to any descendants who may be offended by what I made of him. All that I wrote regarding the conversion of a former priory into what became Newstead Hall is accurate, including the legend of the ghost of the Black Monk. And if the name Byron sounds strangely familiar, that's because when the direct line ran dry in the late eighteenth century, the estate and title fell to a great-nephew, George Gordon, who became the sixth Baron Byron, while devoting his life to poetry and carnal conquests.

These days, Newstead Abbey is on everyone's bucket list for a stately home to visit, and is a popular day out for day-trippers from Nottingham, twelve miles to the south. It is now primarily famous as the former home of the poet Byron, although a brief reference is usually made in the guidebooks to the Black Monk, who Byron actually once encountered and described in one of his lengthy poetic works.

Because of the division of law and order responsibilities between the county and the town, it was necessary, from 1449 onwards, to have separate legal centres for each of them. For the town, at the date of this novel, it was the ancient Guildhall in Weekday Cross, which doubled as what we would call the town hall — the centre of civic government — as well as having its own court and cells. But the other court building to which I made reference has a far more interesting pedigree.

The Shire Hall, as it was called, was the epicentre of law enforcement for the county, and existed as an administrative oasis — a little piece of the county inside the town. It had its own courts, its own bailiff, and in due course its own gallows. It was the location of the county assize court, and as a youth I well recall witnessing the imposition of the death sentence on a murderer. He passed out on the spot, and as an impressionable boy I almost followed him; a place so drenched in misery and past horror can be almost guaranteed to have left a legacy of supernatural atmospherics.

The building has, for the past thirty years, been the location of what is now known as the National Justice Museum, providing the prurient visitor with an insight into what it was like in its former days as a courthouse, complete with condemned cell, exercise yard, gallows socket and instruments of legal persuasion. But high on the list of attractions are the regular ghost tours, because the place has become a particular favourite with paranormal investigation groups who regularly record strange phenomena on their modern equipment, and occasionally encounter ghostly spectres from 'the good old days' of English justice.

The primary theme of the novel is of course the obsession with witchcraft during the dying days of Elizabeth's reign, and the origin of that may be sought in the reign of her father,

Henry VIII. Contrary to popular misconception, Henry did *not* convert England into a Protestant nation. He merely divorced Catholic England from the control of the Pope in Rome, principally so that, as head of the newly formed Church of England, he could grant himself an annulment of his marriage to Katherine of Aragon. The Catholic faith lived on, however, and it was not until the reign of Henry's son and immediate successor, Edward VI, that the 'Reformers' began the process that made England a Protestant nation. By the end of Elizabeth's reign, Rome had lost its influence over Church affairs forever.

But there was a price to pay. It had been the 'old' forms of worship that had kept the Devil from the doorstep, with the Roman traditions of exorcism, prayers for the salvation of souls, intervention by ordained priests and so on. Without them came the revival of fear of the spirits lying behind the shadows, haunting the graveyards, preying on the weak and vulnerable and casting spells on the unprepared and unblessed. Witches had always been feared, but they had been held at bay by prayer, holy water and blessed relics, and now they were free to ride unrestricted through the lives of those upon whom they chose to cast their evil eye.

With the revival of fear of witchcraft came the instant careers of those who claimed to be able to identify witches. Their victims were usually women, since they were held to be the weaker sex, carnally insatiable and the source of sin by men. They were easily seduced by Satan, and they possessed a 'suckling' mark somewhere on their bodies. This was believed to be in the general region of their genitals, entitling lascivious 'witch-finders' to make the necessary examination.

Once an unfortunate local woman — often elderly and living alone — was suspected of being the cause of a poor harvest, a blight among animal herds, an unexplained death or a neighbour's seizure, fear and prejudice took over, and death would follow a farce of a trial that involved the flimsiest of evidence. I made reference to the infamous North Berwick witch trials specifically, since they occurred at the time when King James of Scotland was personally obsessed with witchcraft following an incident at sea that any modern meteorologist could easily explain away. But there were many more like it at that time, and there would be others in the following century, most notoriously in the staunchly Puritan English colony of Massachusetts.

The only truly fictitious characters in this novel were the central ones — Edward, Elizabeth, Francis, Kitty and Rose. I hope you enjoyed reading about their exploits.

As ever, I would be delighted to see a review of my book posted on **Amazon** or **Goodreads**. Alternatively, feel free to visit, and contact me on, my author website: **davidfieldauthor.com**.

Happy reading!

David

Sapere Books is an exciting new publisher of brilliant fiction and popular history.

To find out more about our latest releases and our monthly bargain books visit our website:
saperebooks.com

Printed in Great Britain
by Amazon